A CHILD'S TREASURY OF
CLASSIC STORIES

CHARLES DICKENS ◆ WILLIAM SHAKESPEARE ◆ OSCAR WILDE

RETOLD BY NICOLA BAXTER ◆ ILLUSTRATED BY JENNY THORNE

ARMADILLO

This edition is published by Armadillo,
an imprint of Anness Publishing Ltd,
Blaby Road, Wigston, Leicestershire LE18 4SE

info@anness.com

www.annesspublishing.com

If you like the images in this book and would like to investigate using them for publishing, promotions or advertising, please visit our website www.practicalpictures.com for more information.

Publisher: Joanna Lorenz
Editor: Elizabeth Young
Production Controller: Don Campaniello

Previously published as *Children's Classics*

PUBLISHER'S NOTE
Although the advice and information in this book are believed to be accurate and true at the time of going to press, neither the authors nor the publisher can accept any legal responsibility or liability for any errors or omissions that may have been made.

Manufacturer: Anness Publishing Ltd, Blaby Road, Wigston, Leicestershire LE18 4SE, England
For Product Tracking go to: www.annesspublishing.com/tracking
Batch: 6064-20945-1127

CONTENTS

Stories from
CHARLES DICKENS

INTRODUCTION

Charles Dickens was born on February 7th 1812 in Portsmouth, England, the second of eight children. John Dickens, his father, was a clerk in the Navy Pay Office.

During his childhood, Charles moved house a number of times. In 1817, the Dickens family went to London, but all did not go well there. In 1824, John Dickens was imprisoned for debt in Marshalsea Prison. At the age of twelve, Charles went to work in a blacking factory, earning six shillings a week. It was an experience that contributed greatly to his later views on social reform.

Once his father was free, Charles attended Wellington House Academy, then joined a legal firm before becoming a journalist for the *Morning Chronicle*. In 1836, he married Catherine Hogarth. Already he was more than a reporter. *Sketches by Boz* (1836–37) was followed by the serialization of *The Pickwick Papers*. Then came *Oliver Twist* and *Nicholas Nickleby*. In all he wrote fifteen major novels and countless short stories and articles. As well as writing, he enjoyed travel and amateur theatricals. His marriage ended in 1858. It had not been a happy affair but did produce ten children.

Charles Dickens died at Gad's Hill near Rochester, Kent, on June 9th 1870, aged only 58. He is buried in Poet's Corner in Westminster Abbey. The inscription on his tombstone says, "He was a sympathiser to the poor, the suffering, and the oppressed; and by his death, one of England's greatest writers is lost to the world."

GREAT EXPECTATIONS

My father's family name was Pirrip, and my Christian name Philip. However, all my infant tongue could manage was Pip – and so I came to be called. I never saw my father or my mother. The shape of the letters on my father's tombstone gave me the idea that he was a square, stout man. I imagined my mother freckled and sickly. Ours was marsh country, a dark flat wilderness, near a river and close to the sea.

On a bleak Christmas Eve, I was visiting the graveyard and beginning to cry when a terrible voice cried, "Hold your noise!" and a man started up from between the gravestones. He was a terrible sight, all in coarse grey, with a great iron on his leg.

"You get me a file," he snarled, "and you get me wittles." He ordered me to bring them to the old Battery, early the next morning. "Or I'll have your heart and liver out," he growled.

I ran without stopping to the forge where I lived with my sister and her husband, the blacksmith Joe Gargery. My sister was tall and bony and always wore a coarse apron. Joe was a sweet-tempered, foolish fellow. Wracked with fear, I could only pretend to eat my supper before going up to bed.

Early next morning, I crept downstairs and took from the pantry bread, cheese, mincemeat, brandy and a handsome pork pie. I stole a file from the forge and ran across the marshes towards the old Battery.

Leg irons were often used to restrain prisoners in Victorian times. Convicts were treated very harshly, and it was not uncommon for them to have their legs and arms shackled with rings of iron.

On my way, I observed a man dressed in grey, also with a leg iron, but he quickly vanished. After delivering my stolen goods, I returned home to find visitors arriving for Christmas lunch. There were Mr Hubble the wheelwright and his wife; Mr Wopsle the church clerk, and Joe's uncle, called Mr Pumblechook, a wealthy corn-chandler. I ate in terror of my thefts being noticed.

Then my sister went to get the pork pie.

I left the table and ran to the door – straight into a soldier who held out a pair of broken handcuffs, saying, "Here you are, look sharp."

Joe lit his forge and mended the handcuffs. Then he took me on his back to follow the soldiers. Mr Wopsle also came, and after a chase, two escaped convicts were recaptured.

One was the man from the graveyard and one was the man who had vanished so suddenly. Recognizing me, the convict from the graveyard said, "I took some wittles ... from the blacksmith's ... liquor and a pie."

I watched as the soldiers rowed the captured men out to the waiting hulks. Soon after, I was summoned by Miss Havisham to play with her adopted daughter Estella. Mr Pumblechook took me to Satis House, which was a dismal place. We rang the bell and soon a beautiful young lady appeared. Though about my age, she was as scornful and self-possessed as if she had been twenty-one and a queen.

Hulks were prison ships, made in the hulls of large, unwieldy vessels. Moored off the coast in desolate places, they made a forbidding sight.

She led me through the house, which was devoid of daylight. In a room lit by candles, I met Miss Havisham, sitting by a large dressing table. She was dressed as if for a wedding, in white satin, expensive lace and silk, all turned yellow with age. But she had not quite finished dressing. She wore only one shoe. Her gloves and some jewels lay on the dressing table.

For eight months, I visited Satis House, being taunted by Estella, who taught me how common I was. On Miss Havisham's birthday, I met a burly gentleman of dark complexion, who smelled of soap and wore a large watch-chain.

Miss Havisham showed me a room with a table laid for a wedding feast. Everything was thick with dust, and the mouldy cake was hung with cobwebs. She said, "I will be laid here when I am dead."

Later, a pale young man appeared and asked me to fight. Unwillingly, I agreed and knocked him down.

Eventually Miss Havisham gave me twenty-five guineas and I went to work with Joe and his journeyman Dolge Orlick. I no longer visited Satis House.

Then, one fateful day, my sister was attacked when alone in the house. A tremendous blow to the back of her head sent her out of her wits. Thankfully a neighbour, Biddy, came to tend her.

I was in the fourth year of my apprenticeship when I was approached in the tavern by a lawyer, Mr Jaggers, the burly gentleman I had met at Miss Havisham's house. It seemed that I had come into "great expectations", however, he said, "the name of the person who is your liberal benefactor is to remain a profound secret until the person chooses to reveal it."

*An **apprentice** was a young person being trained by a skilled craftsperson, while a **journeyman** was a craftsman or artisan qualified to work competently at his trade but only under the supervision of an experienced employer.*

I was sure the person must be Miss Havisham. I travelled to London, where I was taken by Wemmick, Mr Jagger's clerk, to Barnard's Inn. Here I lodged with Herbert Pocket, the son of Miss Havisham's brother Matthew. And here I met again the pale youth with whom I had fought.

Herbert told me how Miss Havisham inherited a fortune while her half-brother received much less. I also heard how she fell in love with a man who said he would marry her and then didn't. It was rumoured that he was already married.

Herbert took me to his family home, where I met two fellow students. Startop was kind, with a woman's delicacy of feature, but Bentley Drummle was a sulky fellow, rich, idle, proud and suspicious.

I struck up a friendship with Mr Wemmick, who invited me to his strange, castle-like house to meet his Aged Parent.

Soon after, I had dinner with Mr Jaggers where, as advised by Wemmick, I closely observed Molly the servant. Later, Joe brought a message from Miss Havisham and, when I went to visit, I found Orlick employed as the gate-keeper. Inside I met Estella, now a woman and even more beautiful.

An envelope edged in black brought serious news: my sister had died the previous Monday.

My twenty-first birthday arrived, but my benefactor remained anonymous. I visited Estella at Mrs Bradley's house in Richmond and found Drummle paying court to her.

Years passed, and I was still living the same wasteful, idle life when one stormy night, I heard a noise. I went to the stair-head and held my reading light over the banister. A man approached, dressed roughly like a seaman. He had long, grey hair and was aged about sixty. It was the convict from the graveyard! I was horror-struck to learn that he was my benefactor, not Miss Havisham.

Sentenced to transportation, he had worked and worked to repay me for getting him food and a file.

"You acted nobly, my boy," he said. "I never forgot it." He told me that the other convict I had met on the marshes was called Compeyson. Before long, Herbert and I realized that Compeyson was the evil trickster who had broken Miss Havisham's heart.

Abel Magwitch, my benefactor, was risking his life by returning from transportation. While he hid, I visited Miss Havisham and her ward. I tried to control my trembling voice as I told Estella, "I have loved you long and dearly."

Estella looked at me unmoved. Miss Havisham had taught her to use her beauty to torture men. When I mentioned Drummle's name, she said haughtily, "I am going to be married to him." I covered my face with my hands.

In Victorian times, even minor criminals could be sentenced to **transportation**, *which meant being taken by boat to Australia. Convicts who returned risked being hanged.*

I arrived at the gate of Barnard's Inn to find a note from Wemmick: "*Do not go home.*" He knew I was being watched.

On Wemmick's advice, Herbert took Magwitch to the house of his fiancée at Mill Pond Bank. Meanwhile, I made plans to get Magwitch on a steamer to Europe. Wemmick also explained how Mr Jaggers defended Molly his servant, who was charged with murdering another woman. There was a child and a man involved. I remembered how much Mr Jaggers' servant looked like Estella and was convinced that Molly was Estella's mother.

I visited Miss Havisham. She pleaded with me to forgive her for raising Estelle to have an icy heart, far from her true nature. "Though it be ever so long after my broken heart is dust – pray do it," she begged. I replied, "I can do it now."

Returning from a walk in the garden, I watched the old lady sitting by the fire. Suddenly, a flaming light sprang up, and I saw her running at me, a whirl of fire blazing all around her and soaring above her head. I fought to smother the flames with my coat, then dragged the cloth from the table, scattering the mouldy remains of the wedding feast.

A doctor was called, but it was too late for Miss Havisham. My hands were badly burned, and Herbert took great pains to nurse me. Magwitch was still hiding at Mill Pond Bank, so Herbert and he had talked a great deal about his life. All at once, it became clear to us: Magwitch was Estella's father!

Soon after, I received an anonymous letter, luring me to a little sluice house in the marshes at nine o'clock. It was a trap. I was only saved from being killed by Orlick when Herbert rushed in. Luckily, I had dropped the note and, finding it, he had followed me. Enraged with jealousy, Orlick confessed to killing my sister.

The **Thames** is a tidal river. In Dickens' day, when many boats were still powered by oars or sails, it was important to know the state of the tide before setting out on a journey.

On a March day when the sun shone hot and the wind blew cold, Herbert, Startop and I travelled with Magwitch down the Thames. Herbert and Startop rowed, making good progress with the tide, and we were in position as the steamers approached. Suddenly, a four-oared galley appeared. An official shouted, "You have a returned transport there ... I call upon him to surrender." Amongst others in the galley sat Compeyson. A scuffle ensued, during which Compeyson was drowned and Magwitch was severely injured.

Being ill, Magwitch was allowed a chair in court. The sun came in through the great windows as he was sentenced to be hanged.

I made many petitions for clemency but, as the days passed, Magwitch's health deteriorated. One day I held his hand and told him, "you had a child once.... She is living now. She is a lady and very beautiful. And I love her." He died soon after.

I became ill and regained my senses to find myself being tended by Joe. Slowly I grew stronger, but one morning I rose to find Joe had gone. I followed him back to the forge to discover he and Biddy celebrating their wedding day.

There was nothing left for me at home. My fortune was gone and my friends happily settled. I went abroad for eleven years, working as clerk. When I returned, Biddy and Joe had a son.

On a cold afternoon, I visited Satis House, only to find it utterly demolished. In the desolate garden, I beheld a figure.

"Estella!" I cried.

"I am greatly changed," she warned me. But as I took her hand in mine to leave the ruined place, I saw no shadow of another parting from her.

DAVID
COPPERFIELD

I was born at Blundestone, in Suffolk. My father's eyes had closed upon the light of this world six months before mine opened on it.

On a windy March afternoon before my birth, my mother was sitting by the fire, feeling ill and crying, when a strange woman looked in at the window, pressing her nose against the glass. It was my father's aunt, the rich, eccentric Betsey Trotwood.

Though my father had been a favourite of hers, Aunt Betsey had never met my mother – she had disapproved of my father marrying such a "wax doll". Her arrival caused my mother such a shock that I was born that very Friday. However, when the mild doctor, Mr Chillip, informed Betsey, "It's a boy," she grabbed her bonnet and left without a word.

I was cared for by my mother and the servant Peggotty. With her cheeks and arms so hard and red, I wondered the birds did not peck her in preference to apples. However, the happiness of my childhood was interrupted when Mr Murdstone began to pay court to my mother.

One day Peggotty took me to visit her family in Yarmouth. I met her brother Daniel and his adopted nephew and niece, Ham and Little Em'ly, who, along with the widow Mrs Gummage, lived in a large black barge on the beach. It had an iron funnel sticking out for a chimney and a door cut in the side. I quite fell in love with the beautiful Em'ly, who told me as we walked along the beach, "I should like so much to be a lady."

Barges *were sturdy vessels designed to carry cargo safely. In Victorian times, many trading companies used boats to move goods up and down the coast.*

On a cold, grey afternoon, I returned home to find my mother had married Mr Murdstone. Soon Mr Murdstone's sister Jane came to live with us, too. Murdstone was a cruel, unfeeling man. One day, when he beat me for not learning my lessons well enough, I caught the hand with which he held me in my mouth and closed my teeth firmly around it. Despite my mother's protestations, I was dispatched to Salem House, a boarding school in London.

Mr Barkis took me part of the way in his cart, asking me that when I wrote to Peggotty I should give her the strange message, "*Barkis is willin.*"

Salem House was run by Mr Creakle, a friend of cold Mr Murdstone. On arrival, I found myself forced to wear a sign proclaiming: *Take care of him. He bites.* I would have been miserable had it not been for the good hearted Tommy Traddles and the handsome, confident James Steerforth.

When the holidays arrived, I again travelled with Barkis, who was sad that Peggotty had not responded. You might tell her, he said to me, "Barkis was 'a waitin' for an answer."

It felt strange to be home and discover my mother sitting by the fire, suckling an infant. She and Peggotty kissed me repeatedly. Mr Murdstone and Jane remained aloof.

I was soon sent back to school, which continued unchanged until the day I was called into Mr Creakle's office. "Your mother…," he said, "is very … ill … she is … dead."

On my way home, I stopped in Yarmouth to be measured for my mourning clothes. Mr Omer, the undertaker, was a jolly man, cheerfully assisted by his daughter Minnie and his coffin-maker, called Joram.

Mourning, in Dickens' day, had a formal aspect. It was common to have special black clothes made for it. As a mark of respect, people would often wear black for a year or more after a loved one had died.

Back home, a distraught Peggotty told me, "She was never well for a long time." The baby had also died.

Discharged from service, Peggotty took me to visit Yarmouth again. In a small church, she quietly married the faithful Barkis.

I did not return to school but was sent to the Murdstone & Grinby counting-house in Blackfriars. Here I met Mr Micawber, who rented me a room. I soon became friends with his wife and children.

*Victorians who fell into debt could be sent to a **debtor's prison**. These were terrible places from which people could only be freed once the debt was paid – an almost impossible task unless the prisoner had wealthy friends to help.*

Mr Micawber was a stoutish, middle-aged man, with no more hair on his large and shining head than there is upon an egg. He was perpetually in debt and was eventually sent to prison.

On his release, Mr Micawber decided to leave London with his family. I used guile to get Peggotty to send me money and Aunt Betsy's address in Dover. Though my belongings and money were stolen on the way, I continued my journey on foot, arriving with my clothes and shoes in a woeful condition. Finding my aunt in her neat cottage garden, I announced, "If you please, Aunt, I am your nephew."

"Oh Lord!" said my Aunt, and sat down on the gravel path. But she let me stay, especially after meeting Mr Murdstone and Miss Murdstone, who rode a donkey across my aunt's beloved green!

I liked living with my strange, eccentric aunt and would often fly a kite with her companion, the child-like Mr Dick.

One day, my aunt took me to Canterbury. Inside a very old house with long, low, lattice-windows, I met her lawyer, Mr Wickfield, his dutiful daughter Agnes and his curious-looking clerk Uriah Heep, a high-shouldered, bony youth with red hair cropped like stubble, hardly any eyelashes and no eyebrows.

Waiting for my aunt, I sat opposite the room where Uriah worked. His eyes, like two red suns, observed me stealthily. On Mr Wickfield's advice, I lodged with him while attending a school run by the kind Dr. Strong.

When I had completed my education, my aunt gave me leave to visit Peggotty while I considered a suitable career. In London I met Steerforth, who took me to Highgate to meet his proud, possessive mother and her companion, Rosa Dartle. Rosa had a scar across her lips. "I was a young boy, and she exasperated me, and I threw a hammer at her," explained Steerforth.

I, in turn, took Steerforth to visit the Peggottys. Ham and Little Em'ly had just become engaged. Steerforth liked Yarmouth so much he bought a boat, so he could sail there regularly.

Back in London once more, I was apprenticed to Spenlow & Jorkins. One evening, I met Agnes, who was visiting London to see her father's agent. She warned me against Steerforth and told me that Uriah was "subtle and watchful. He has mastered Papa's weaknesses," she said, "and taken advantage of them." Talking to me soon after, Uriah confided his passion for Agnes. I was horrified.

But passion was soon to enter my own life. On meeting Mr Spenlow's silly but beautiful daughter Dora, I fell hopelessly in love. She had the most delightful voice, the gayest laugh, the most fascinating ways. Unfortunately, her father had engaged Miss Murdstone as a companion for his daughter.

One evening, as I was dining with the Micawbers and my old school-friend Tommy Traddles, Steerforth brought a note from Peggotty. Barkis was dying. Naturally, I hurried to Yarmouth.

I was to find that soon after Barkis's death, Em'ly disappeared, leaving Ham a note in which she vowed "never to come back, unless he brings me back a lady." The man involved was Steerforth. Distraught, Peggotty's brother Daniel set off to search for Em'ly, saying, "My unchanged love is with my darling child, and I forgive her."

Back in London, my aunt arrived, claiming that her investments had failed and she and Mr Dick must live with me. Later, when I visited Canterbury, Agnes revealed that Uriah was now Mr Wickfield's business partner. No longer a humble clerk, he had moved, with his mother, into the Wickfields' house.

Poor as I was, I had been courting Dora in secret. When Mrs Murdstone showed my love letters to Dora's father, he vehemently disapproved. However, when he died suddenly, leaving Dora penniless, she was sent to live with her aunts. Eventually, we were married. Beautiful, silly Dora attempted to keep house for me but was totally inept.

On a visit to Canterbury, I found Mr Micawber working for Uriah, who had virtually taken over the business. I begged Agnes not to marry Uriah just to please her father, who was depressed and drinking heavily.

Back in London once more, I met Daniel Peggotty, newly returned from Europe and still resolutely searching for Em'ly. Later, Steerforth's manservant told me how Steerforth had abandoned Em'ly. Led by Martha to a dingy attic room, Daniel Peggotty at last found his Em'ly. "I thank my Heav'nly Father as my dream's come true," he cried, taking her up in his arms. At once he began to make plans to emigrate to Australia, where Em'ly's past would be unknown.

Dora was gravely ill, but she insisted I go to witness Traddles and Mr Micawber confronting Uriah. While working for Uriah, Mr Micawber had discovered how the former clerk had tricked Mr Wickfield into signing over control of the firm.

Embezzlement *is when money or property is entrusted to someone who does not own it, but who fraudulently makes use of it for their own ends.*

Uriah had forged Wickfield's signature and framed him for embezzlement. Aunt Betsy waded into the fray, grabbing Uriah, "You know what I want," she shouted. She had feared Mr Wickfield had embezzled her money but had kept quiet for the sake of Agnes. Now Mr Wickfield's name was cleared and Aunt Betsy recovered her investments. She kindly lent the Micawbers enough money to make a fresh start in Australia.

Back in London, Agnes was with Dora when she died. Darkness came before my eyes. It felt as if my whole world had ended.

I agreed to take a letter from Em'ly to Ham, but arrived in Yarmouth to find a storm raging and a schooner about to be wrecked on the beach. Unconcerned for his own life, Ham waded into the waves and died attempting to save a stranger, who also died. The stranger was Steerforth.

*A **schooner** is a sailing vessel with two masts or more. They were used to transport goods such as fruit from Portugal and sherry from Spain.*

The Micawbers and the Peggottys, including Mrs Gummage and Martha, set sail for Australia. I spent some time in Switzerland, writing about my experiences. I often thought about Agnes, too.

At last, I returned to Dover, where my aunt gave me news of all my old friends and told me she suspected Agnes had an attachment. I called on Agnes and, as we spoke of Dora and Em'ly, I noticed how beautiful she was. Eventually I told her, "I went away, dear Agnes, loving you. I stayed away, loving you. I returned home, loving you." She laid her gentle hands on my shoulders and looked at me calmly. "I have loved you all my life," she said.

OLIVER TWIST

In a workhouse, in an unnamed English town, a child was born into a world of sorrow. His young, unmarried mother died before she could give him a name or tell anyone hers. Named by the authorities, Oliver Twist was sent to the parish baby farm to endure nine years of hunger and harshness until Mr Bumble, the parish beadle, returned him to the workhouse.

Food was scarce in the workhouse, and when Oliver asked bravely, "Please Sir, I want some more," he was punished severely.

Five pounds was offered to anyone who would take Oliver as an apprentice. Cruel Mr Gamfield, the chimney sweep, applied but was rejected when the half-blind magistrate noticed Oliver's terror.

Eventually, Oliver was apprenticed to Mr Sowerberry, the undertaker. There he met cruel Noah Claypole and the servant girl Charlotte, who was in love with Noah. Oliver was fed with cold bits put by for the dog. Worse still was his nightly feeling of awe and dread – for he had to sleep among unfinished coffins.

Workhouses *were places where the poor did unpaid work in exchange for food and accommodation. There, conditions were harsh, and families were often split up.*

Oliver had to work as a mourner. His pale, melancholy face proved especially useful for children's funerals. Noah was a bully and said cruel things about Oliver's mother. A fight began, causing Mrs Sowerberry to lock Oliver in the coal cellar and send Noah for Mr Bumble. "It's not Madness, ma'am ... it's Meat," claimed Mr Bumble, implying that Oliver was being treated too well.

Upset and angry, Oliver ran away. As he passed the workhouse, he met a dying child called Dick. "God bless you," said the poor boy – the first good wishes Oliver had ever received.

Arriving in London, exhausted and penniless, Oliver met another boy – the roistering, swaggering Artful Dodger, who took him to an old man called Fagin who seemed to have care of several boys. Warm, well fed and lulled by hot gin and water, Oliver slept deeply. He awoke to see Fagin gloating over a secret hoard of treasure. Noticing Oliver was awake, Fagin grabbed a knife as if to silence the boy for ever. Luckily, the old man calmed down. Later, Fagin taught his boys to pick pockets.

After much practice, Oliver was sent out with Charlie and Dodger, who picked the pocket of a gentleman reading at a book stall. Shocked, Oliver ran. The gentleman missed his handkerchief and cried, "Stop thief!" A chase began, in which Charlie and Dodger gleefully took part! Oliver was knocked down, but the gentleman took pity on him and went with him to the police station.

Oliver was locked in a filthy cell. Mr Brownlow, the gentleman, felt that he had seen Oliver before but he could not recall where.

When Oliver was brought before the rude and incompetent magistrate Fang, he was too afraid to speak. Just in time, the bookseller rushed in, saying that Oliver was not the thief. So it was that Oliver went home with Mr Brownlow and was cared for by his kindly housekeeper, Mrs Bedwin. The boy became fascinated by a portrait hanging in his bedroom. Mr Brownlow was amazed to see the likeness between Oliver and the woman in the portrait.

Fagin and his friend Bill Sikes, who made his living robbing houses, discussed recapturing Oliver – Bill's girlfriend Nancy was at the magistrate's office and observed the trial.

Back at Mr Brownlow's, the portrait had been removed, and Oliver was happy. When Mr Brownlow had books to be returned to the bookseller, Oliver begged, "Do let me take them! I'll run all the way."

In Clerkenwell, Oliver turned down a by-street and was grabbed by Nancy. A crowd gathered. "Thank gracious goodness heavins, I've found him!" cried Nancy, claiming Oliver as her brother.

*In Victorian times, many working-class people could not read or write. A **book stall** would be a good place to find well-to-do people with pockets ripe for picking.*

Returned to Fagin and Sikes, Oliver feared Mr Brownlow would think him a thief, but the gang just laughed. Oliver tried to run, and was saved from being savaged by Sikes's dog when Nancy screamed, "Keep back the dog ... the child shan't be torn down by the dog unless you kill me first."

Oliver was caught, but Nancy grabbed the club with which Fagin began to beat him. The brutal Sikes wrestled with Nancy until she passed out.

Mr Brownlow did not forget Oliver. On a visit to London, Mr Bumble the beadle spied a newspaper advertisement offering five guineas for information about Oliver Twist. He called on Mr Brownlow and told many lies about Oliver.

Meanwhile, Fagin and Sikes decided Oliver should help with a robbery. On a cold, rainy morning, Oliver and Sikes trudged west through London to meet Toby Crackit and Barney. Oliver was lifted through the small window of an elegant house. He meant to raise the alarm, but two servants appeared inside and Oliver was shot. Sikes dragged him back through the window, and they ran.

Back at the workhouse, Mr Bumble was about to propose to Mrs Corney, the workhouse matron, when she was summoned to the deathbed of Old Sally, who tended Oliver's mother when she died. Sally confessed that Oliver's mother had saved some gold with which to buy him some "friends". "I robbed her, so I did. She wasn't cold – I tell you she wasn't cold, when I stole it," cried Sally.

Back at Fagin's house, Toby Crackit returned from the failed robbery. When Fagin learned that Sikes had abandoned Oliver in a ditch, he rushed to the Three Cripples tavern. Barney had not returned either.

Fagin found Nancy, who appeared to have been drinking heavily. He raged about Oliver being worth hundreds of pounds. Nancy pretended not to understand, saying Oliver was "better where he is, than among us."

Fagin went home, where he found a man waiting for him. This nervous character was called Monks and appeared to have an interest in the fate of Oliver Twist. It seemed that he wanted the boy to be out of the way but did not wish him dead.

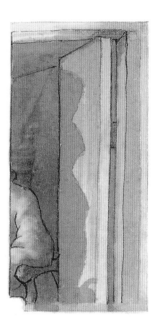

*In Dickens' lifetime **drunkenness** was a problem for men and women. Throughout London's slums, gin and ale were cheap and readily available.*

As day dawned, Oliver climbed from his ditch with a cry of pain. His left arm, bandaged in a shawl, hung useless at his side. The shawl was saturated with blood.

The desperate boy staggered towards a house, only to faint on the doorstep. It was the house of the robbery, and the servants recognized Oliver, but Mrs Maylie and her niece Rose, who lived there, were kind to him.

Beautiful Rose Maylie was seventeen. She insisted that Oliver should be carried up to bed and that Dr. Losberne should be summoned.

Later that day Oliver told his story. Convinced of his innocence, Dr. Losberne persuaded the servant Giles that the thief he shot was not Oliver. Just then, the Bow Street Runners arrived, but they were unable to solve the crime. When Oliver felt better, Dr. Losberne took him to see Mr Brownlow. On the way, Oliver recognized the house where the robbers met before the robbery. Dr. Losberne spoke to a man there, asking for Sikes by name. He left without success, but not before the man had caught a glimpse of Oliver.

The Bow Street Runners were a semi-official group organized in the mid-eighteenth century. Their primary role was finding and arresting robbers. In 1839, they were replaced by a professional police force.

When Oliver and Dr. Losberne arrived back in London, they found that Mr Brownlow had left for the West Indies.

With continued kindness, the Maylies took Oliver with them when they moved into the countryside. In this idyllic setting, however, Rose fell ill and Oliver was asked to send a letter summoning Dr. Losberne. On his way home, Oliver had a disturbing encounter with a man who looked into his eyes and cried, "Death!"

Fortunately, Rose recovered. Mrs Maylie's son Henry arrived, declaring his love for Rose, but Mrs Maylie feared that "youth has many generous impulses which do not last."

Henry, who was running for parliament with the help of his powerful uncle, asked Rose to marry him. Rose feared that her past would hinder his career and so refused. When Henry left, he asked Oliver to write to him every fortnight.

Sitting over his books one night, Oliver awoke from a nightmare to see Fagin at the window. With him was the man who had cried, "Death!" Oliver raised the alarm, but, though they searched, the Maylie household could find no evidence of Fagin's visit.

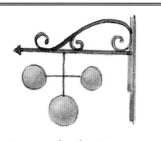

*A **pawnbroker** is a person who lends money. Personal property of a similar value is left as security. The property can be sold if the loan and interest are not repaid within the specified time.*

Back at the workhouse, Mr Bumble met Monks in a tavern and, in a crumbling building by a river, Mrs Bumble made Monks pay twenty-five sovereigns before she would speak of Oliver's origins.

She described how, when Old Sally died, she took the pawnbroker's ticket out of her hand and redeemed a beautiful gold locket containing two hairs and a wedding ring engraved with "Agnes" and a date within a year of Oliver's birth. Monks took the jewellery and, opening a trapdoor, dropped them into the raging river below.

Later, as Fagin and Monks whispered together, Nancy eavesdropped. Shocked by what she heard, she drugged Sikes with laudanum and went to see Rose.

Nancy told Rose that Monks knew of Oliver's parentage and destroyed the evidence to be sure he got an inheritance – for Monks was Oliver's half-brother. Refusing money from Rose, Nancy hurried home, terrified that Sikes would have discovered her missing.

The following day, Rose, Mrs Maylie, Henry, Mr Brownlow, and Dr. Losberne decided to secure Oliver his inheritance.

Nancy tried to meet Rose once more, this time on London Bridge. Fagin was suspicious and had Nancy followed. When Sikes was told of what he saw as Nancy's treachery, he rushed home and beat his pistol on her upturned face. Almost blind with blood, Nancy held Rose's white handkerchief to heaven, praying for mercy. Sikes murdered her with a club – even his dog's paws became bloody.

Confronted by Mr Brownlow, Monks revealed himself to be Edward Leeford, the son of Mr Brownlow's oldest friend. This friend was forced into an unhappy marriage, which produced Monks. Later he met Agnes, whom he hoped to marry, but he died while she was pregnant. No will was found, so his estate went to his first wife.

When Mr Brownlow first rescued Oliver, he had no idea of his identity. It was the picture of Agnes left by his friend that gave him a clue.

Two days later, Oliver went back to his birthplace, where he met his half-brother Monks. When Mr Leeford died, Monks's mother had destroyed the letter he left for Agnes, Oliver's mother, explaining he was already married – albeit unhappily. Monks's mother had also destroyed the will naming Oliver as heir. The discovery was made that Rose was Oliver's mother's younger sister, the boy's aunt.

Unfortunately for Oliver, his dear friend Dick had died, but with the mysteries all solved, the Bumbles lost their jobs and, though Monks escaped from England, he died in a New World prison. Sikes, too, met his death as he tried to escape across the rooftops. Henry Maylie, now a curate, married Rose at last. As befits someone so evil, Fagin was tried and condemned to hang, while Oliver lived happily and peacefully amongst his friends in the countryside.

THE OLD
CURIOSITY
SHOP

While walking through the dark streets of London one night, taking pleasure in speculating about the people he saw around him, an infirm old man was approached by a pretty little girl who was lost. Her name was Nell Trent. The old man, whose name was Master Humphrey, helped her back to her home, which turned out to be a shop filled with old and curious things: suits of armour, fantastic carvings, rusty weapons, furniture, and figures in china, wood, iron and ivory.

At the strange shop, Master Humphrey met Nell's grandfather, who clearly adored her. He also made the acquaintance of Kit Nubbles, an honest lad equally devoted to the little girl. As Master Humphrey left, Nell's grandfather also went out into the night.

A week later, the old man returned to the shop. Interrupting a boisterous debate inside, he found Nell's brother Fred and Fred's friend Richard Swiveller. Nell was out but soon arrived with one

THE OLD CURIOSITY SHOP · 45

Daniel Quilp, a short, elderly man with restless, sly eyes and an unwholesome complexion. Quilp lived at Tower Hill, where his wife and his mother-in-law, Mrs Jiniwin, suffered cruelly at his hands.

One day, Nell took a letter from her grandfather to Quilp at his wharf. Quilp seemed perplexed by its contents and frightened Nell by suggesting that she should become "Mrs Quilp the second, when Mrs Quilp the first is dead".

A **wharf** is a sturdy platform built by the side of a harbour or river. It is used for the loading and unloading of boats and for the storage of goods.

Quilp took Nell back to his home and listened behind the door while the girl confided to Mrs Quilp that her grandfather went out of the house each night. Nell explained that her beloved grandfather seemed like a different person now. "We were once so happy and he so cheerful and contented!" she said in distress. "You cannot think what a sad change has fallen on us, since."

Quilp was not the only one to have designs on Little Nell. At Fred's lodgings, he and Richard discussed Richard marrying her. They believed her grandfather was rich and wanted a share of the fortune.

Just three nights after Nell's confession to Mrs Quilp, her grandfather, who had been ill all day, said he would not be going out that night. Suddenly, Quilp appeared, crying, "You have no secret from me now." He had discovered that Nell's grandfather had been gambling and claimed it was the faithful Kit who told him.

In fact, Kit was at his usual post, standing in the shadow of an archway in the street outside and keeping a watch over the comings and goings at the shop until Little Nell was safely in bed.

Daniel Quilp's evil actions were not without consequences for Kit. When he was back at his home, Nell arrived with some money. Her grandfather, she said, had had some kind of fit and discharged Kit from his service. "He complains and raves of you," said Nell.

Now the coast was clear, Quilp and his lawyer, Sampson Brass, took up residence in the curiosity shop. But Kit was worried about Nell and took every opportunity to try to see her, often being turned away from the door. Eventually, he managed to have a word and offered her the front room upstairs in his house as a refuge. "Mother says it would be just the thing for you," he said.

Quilp's plans were foiled, however, when, on a June morning, Nell stole the key from Quilp and escaped with her grandfather. They had nowhere to go and became beggars.

Nell was particularly sad to leave her pet bird, a linnet, behind. After she left, Kit fought Tom, Quilp's wharf boy, for the bird.

Searching for work, Kit Nubbles met a Mr and Mrs Garland on their way to see Mr Witherden, the notary. They had no change, so gave Kit a shilling for holding their horse, when the usual rate was sixpence (half a shilling).

Punch and Judy *was (and still is) a puppet show that probably originated in Italy. Although it is usually seen as a children's entertainment, the show is very violent, with Punch attacking his wife and baby.*

In a nearby graveyard, Nell and her grandfather met Short Trotters and Tommy Codlin the Punch men. "Look," said Tommy, "here's Judy's clothes falling to pieces again. You haven't got a needle and thread, I suppose?" Nell helped to mend Judy and secretly sewed a gold coin into her own dress. Nell and the old man travelled with the Punch men, but by the time they reached the races, Nell was feeling uneasy. While a show was in progress, the pair made their escape.

*In Victorian times, a **notary** was an official authorized to prepare legal documents. He also had the power to administer oaths.*

When Nell had been gone a week, Kit was still hopeful she would soon return. He went to the notary to work off the other half of his shilling, and ended up being hired by Mr and Mrs Garland of Abel Cottage, Finchley. Here he met a servant-girl called Barbara.

Meanwhile, Quilp and Richard Swiveller went together to the Wilderness tavern, and the evil Quilp agreed to help Richard marry Nell, knowing that her grandfather had no fortune.

Nell and her grandfather had been lucky to meet and stay with a kindly schoolmaster. Next day he said, "You're very welcome to pass another night here. I should be really glad if you would." It so happened that while the visitors were there, the schoolmaster's favourite pupil died.

Nell and her grandfather continued their journey, joining up with Mrs Jarley and George, who owned a travelling waxworks show. Nell secured a job showing visitors around the waxworks. One evening, Nell caught sight of Quilp, but luckily he did not see her. Later, out for a walk, she and her grandfather were caught in a violent storm. As they sheltered at the Valiant Soldier tavern, Nell's grandfather began to gamble, losing everything that was left in Nell's purse.

They stayed the night, paying with the coin sewn into Nell's dress. While the distressed girl was in bed, a creature entered her room. Silently and stealthily, it stole the change from the coin. The robber was her grandfather, but next morning Nell could not get

him to confess. At the waxworks once more, Nell's grandfather went out late at night and returned penniless but still determined to gamble. He believed he must do it to secure Nell's future.

Back in London, Quilp persuaded Sampson Brass and his sister Sally to take on Richard Swiveller as a clerk. Richard was alone in the office when a little voice from very low down said, "Oh please, will you come and show the lodgings?" It was a servant-girl in a coarse, dirty apron. Shown the lodgings, a single gentleman brought up his trunk, paid and went to bed in the middle of the day. It was impossible to wake him. The new lodger later revealed a special interest in Punch shows, eventually meeting Short Trotters and Tommy Codlin. He gave them each a sovereign, promising if Nell was found, it was "but a prelude to twenty more".

On the quarter day, Kit and Barbara got a half-day holiday and so gathered with their mothers and Kit's two younger brothers for tea at Kit's mother's house. They watched a play and ate oysters. To Barbara's annoyance, Kit spoke repeatedly of Nell's beauty.

Next day, Kit had to go to the notary's – the mysterious lodger had found Nell. Afraid to upset his old master, Kit refused to go but suggested his mother went instead.

Far away, Nell's grandfather was still gambling. Nell observed him with some gypsies, who suggested he stole the waxwork takings. Nell told him she had had a terrible dream. "I have had it once before," she said. "It is a dream of grey-haired men like you, in darkened rooms by night, robbing sleepers of their gold. Up! ... Nothing but flight can save us."

Arriving in a filthy, industrial town, Nell and her grandfather were helped by a stranger, miserably clad and begrimed with smoke. He took them to a foundry, where they were able to sleep on a heap of warm ashes. Next day, their money ran out. "Charity! A morsel of bread!" begged Nell, but the people had nothing to give. She fainted from weakness.

The schoolmaster, who was travelling to a new employer, carried Nell to an inn and summoned a doctor. When she had recovered, Nell and her grandfather went with the schoolmaster by stage wagon to a peaceful, country place.

By the time Kit's mother and the gentleman lodger reached the waxworks, Nell was not there. In an inn, Kit's mother and the gentleman met Quilp.

Dissatisfied, the parties returned home, but while Kit welcomed his mother with open arms, Quilp arrived to find his wife, his mother-in-law and Sampson Brass drinking his spirits in the belief that he was dead. Only Tom the wharf boy was pleased to see him.

Nell, her grandfather and the schoolmaster arrived at their destination, a village with thatched cottages, a stream and the blue Welsh mountains just visible far away. Here they met the clergyman, and Nell was employed to caretake the church.

Back in London, whenever Kit brought a message, Sampson Brass sent Richard on an errand and gave Kit some money, saying it was from the gentleman lodger. One day, Richard went downstairs and played cards with the small servant, whom he liked and named "the Marchioness".

When Sally claimed a silver pencilcase and a knife were missing, Sampson said he was also missing some money. He placed a five-pound note on his desk. Kit arrived, and Sampson insisted he put down his hat. As Sampson was speaking, he moved the hat once or twice. Then he asked, "Will you mind the office one minute, while I run upstairs?" Later, the note was found in Kit's hat. He was arrested.

Quilp made Sampson fire Richard. Shortly afterwards, Richard developed a raging fever. The small servant girl escaped the Brass household and for three weeks tenderly nursed him. When he recovered, he asked her, "What has become of Kit?" Afraid to make him ill again, the girl told how she overheard Sampson and Sally plotting to put the money in Kit's hat. The cowardly Sampson was tricked into confessing his evil deeds, but Sally slipped quietly away. She sent a note warning Quilp, who, trying to escape from the wharf in thick fog, stumbled into the water and was drowned.

*A **sexton** was a man employed to take care of a church. His role was a varied one, often including digging graves and bell-ringing.*

At a reception held to celebrate Kit's release, Mr Garland revealed that his brother was a friend of the clergyman in the country. Mr Garland, Kit and the gentleman lodger set off through the snow to find Nell. During the journey, the gentleman revealed that he was the younger brother of Nell's grandfather. Arriving after midnight, they had to wake the sexton and ask him to point out the right house.

Kit opened a door to see a man sitting with bowed head by the dull, red glow of a fire. No lamp or candle was lit. Kit recognized his old master. The visitors gently approached Nell, lying on her bed. Hoping to please her, Kit had brought the linnet. However, although her grandfather was too confused to know it, Nell was not asleep. She was dead, having passed away two days before.

A local child took Nell's grandfather for a walk while Nell was being buried. The vault was covered, and the stone fixed down. When the old man returned, he searched in vain, calling pitifully for Nell. When told she was dead, he fell down like a murdered man. There seemed little chance of him surviving, but eventually he pulled through. He began to go each day to wait for Nell at her grave. On a genial day in spring he was found dead on her stone, and was laid in the earth by her side.

With Nell and her grandfather both dead, Sampson Brass was found guilty of numerous crimes. However, because he co-operated with the police, he escaped transportation and was merely imprisoned. Some rumours said that his sister became a sailor, some said a soldier who could be seen standing to attention in St. James's Park. Many believed that both Sampson and Sally ended up as vagrants.

Daniel Quilp's body was recovered and a verdict of suicide returned. Only Tom the wharf boy cried at the inquest. Mrs Quilp remarried and set out to enjoy her first husband's money. The Garlands continued to live at Abel Cottage.

Unfortunately, Nell's brother Fred drowned in France. Having been left an annual allowance in his rich aunt's will, Richard Swiveller educated and then married the Marchioness. The schoolmaster stayed in his idyllic country spot, and the gentleman lodger, although filled with sadness by the course that events had taken, took great delight in retracing the steps of Nell and her grandfather and being kind to those who had been kind to them.

Kit found a new position, and his mother and brothers were secured from want and made quite happy. Kit did not remain a single man all his life but eventually married Barbara. Together they had children of their own, much to the delight of both mothers, and often Kit gathered them to him and told them of good Miss Nell who died. When they cried to hear the tale of woe, he reminded them that she had gone to heaven and that they would go there too if they were good. In heaven he assured them, everyone would be happy, and they would know Nell as he had done as a boy.

Sometimes he took the little ones to the street where Nell had lived. However, time had passed, and the house that once held all the old curious things, the suits of armour, fantastic carvings, rusty weapons, furniture, figures in china, iron and ivory, had been pulled down. Soon Kit could no longer be certain of the spot where the shop had stood.

Such are the changes that a few years bring about, and so do things pass away, like a tale that is told …

NICHOLAS NICKLEBY

Ralph Nickleby lived in Golden Square, London. His neighbours believed him rich, though none quite knew how he earned his money. He had cold, restless eyes.

One day, as he was returning home from a meeting, Ralph was met by Newman Noggs, his assistant, a tall man of middle age with a false eye. He handed Ralph an envelope edged in black – Ralph's brother had died, leaving his family penniless. Not at all upset, Ralph called on his brother's widow and her children, called Nicholas and Kate. They had travelled up from Devon and were lodging at the house of Miss La Creevy in the Strand.

Appealed to for help, Ralph Nickleby showed Nicholas an advertisement for an assistant at Mr Wackford Squeers' school, Dotheboys Hall, in Yorkshire, claiming "let him get that situation and his fortune is made." Hesitant at first, Nicholas eventually replied, "I am ready to do anything you wish me. Let us try our fortune with Mr Squeers at once."

A **trunk** *is a large, strong box, used when travelling. It might contain clothes or books. A deal trunk was an inexpensive one made of planks of pine.*

Near Smithfield Market was the Saracen's Head Inn. At half past three one afternoon, a small, unhappy looking boy was sitting on a deal trunk in the Coffee Room. By him was Mr Wackford Squeers, dressed in a suit of scholastic black. He had but one eye, and the blank side of his face was much wrinkled. His appearance was sinister, especially when he smiled. As he was speaking to Mr Snawley, who was considering sending his two stepsons to Dotheboys, Ralph entered, offering the services of his nephew Nicholas, "hot from school, with everything he learned there fermenting in his head, and nothing fermenting in his pocket," Squeers considered, then turned to Nicholas, who had accompanied his uncle, and said, "Your uncle's recommendation has done it." Nicholas was hired.

Ralph sent Nicholas home to pack, giving him some documents and saying, "Leave these papers with my clerk."

In Golden Square, Newman Noggs turned very pale when Nicholas announced he was going to Dotheboys. Nicholas's gentle sister Kate had her doubts as well. When she met Mr Squeers, she asked her brother, "What kind of place can it be that you are going to?" But Nicholas was decided.

As he climbed into the stagecoach that would take him to the school, Nicholas called to his mother, "Bless you, love, and goodbye." When no one was looking, Newman Noggs secretly handed the young man a note, mysteriously whispering, "Take it. Read it. Nobody knows."

Nicholas travelled with Mr Squeers and some boys on their way to become pupils at Dotheboys. The journey to Yorkshire was harsh, but eventually they arrived at a long, cold-looking house, one storey high, with a few straggling outbuildings behind. A strange, tall boy, whom Nicholas learnt was named Smike, opened the yard gate and stepped forward with a lamp.

Later, Nicholas ate a frugal supper with Mr and Mrs Squeers and soon met their daughter Fanny and their son Wackford.

That night, as he prepared for bed, Nicholas opened the letter from Newman. Because Nicholas's father had once helped him, Newman was offering assistance to Nicholas, should he ever need it.

Back in London, Kate was sitting for Miss La Creevy, who painted miniatures, when Ralph arrived. He had found work for Kate with the milliner Madame Mantalini. Though not the position she had hoped for, Kate said, "I am very much obliged to you, uncle."

Ralph had also arranged new lodgings for his relatives. Newman took Kate and Mrs Nickleby to rooms in a dingy house in Thames Street. "This house depresses and chills one," shivered Kate, "as if some blight had fallen on it."

Although poor himself, Newman Noggs had done his best, organizing some furniture, milk for tea, and coal for the women.

Miniatures *are very small, intricate paintings. During the Victorian period, portraits in this style were immensely popular, painted in oils or other mediums.*

Unaware of all this, Nicholas was learning the full horrors of Dotheboys Hall. The schoolroom was bare and dirty, its broken windows stopped up with old copybooks. The ill-treated pupils were thin, with the faces of old men darkened by suffering and neglect. When Smike asked, "is the world as bad and dismal as this place?" Nicholas Nickleby replied, "its hardest, coarsest toil were happiness to this."

Having fallen in love with Nicholas, Fanny Squeers arranged a tea party, where Nicholas met Fanny's friend Matilda and Matilda's fiancé, the large Yorkshireman John Browdie. Nicholas's feelings were confused, but he later told Fanny that he had "not one thought wish or hope" of affection for her. Fanny was very distressed by this declaration.

The miserable life at Dotheboys Hall continued. One freezing January morning, Smike was found to be missing. Mr and Mrs Squeers scoured the countryside until he was recaptured. With the whole school assembled, Mr Squeers began to beat Smike.

"Stop!" cried Nicholas in a voice that made the rafters ring. "This must not go on."

Aghast, Squeers released Smike. Then, in a violent outbreak of wrath and with a cry like the howl of a wild beast, Squeers spat at Nicholas and struck him across the face. Concentrating all his feelings of rage, scorn and indignation, Nicholas sprang upon Squeers, wrestling the cane from his hand and grabbing him by the throat before beating the ruffian until he roared for mercy.

Nicholas left the school on foot. On the way, he met John Browdie, who congratulated him on what he had done. Next morning he awoke in a barn. Smike, who had followed him, dropped to his knees, begging, "take me with you, pray." "Come," said Nicholas.

Newman Noggs was with his friends the Kenwigs when Nicholas and Smike arrived from Yorkshire, exhausted. A letter had already been sent from Fanny Squeers to Ralph, but luckily Ralph was away.

Staying with Newman but in urgent need of work, Nicholas went to the General Agency Office, where he saw a pretty girl, neatly attired, accompanied by a slovenly, red-faced girl. He refused work with a corrupt MP.

Unaware that Nicholas was in London, Kate was unhappy working at Madame Mantalini's. One evening Ralph invited her to supper at his

*A **General Agency Office** was a place where employers could advertise for servants such as cooks, butlers, secretaries or parlour maids, and people with skills to offer could advertise for work. Today it might be called an Employment Agency.*

house, saying, "Come in a hackney coach. I'll pay. Good night … a … a … God bless you." Somehow the blessing seemed to stick in his throat. Mrs Nickleby was excited about her daughter's invitation, so Kate was ready in her black silk dress long before the ordered carriage arrived.

At Golden Square, Ralph took his niece into an opulent room where some gentlemen were gathered. They were introduced to her as Mr Pluck, Mr Pyke, Sir Mulberry Hawk and Lord Frederick Verisopht, who said, "devilish pretty" on sight of her.

At dinner, Kate had to sit between Lord Frederick and Sir Mulberry. When Sir Mulberry behaved cruelly, Kate rushed out. Sir Mulberry followed her upstairs. When Kate attempted to escape, he grabbed her dress. "Unhand me, sir, this instant!" cried Kate. "Not for the world!" was the aristocrat's evil reply.

"What is this?" demanded Ralph, appearing in the doorway. Taking Sir Mulberry to one side, Ralph confessed, "As a matter of business I thought she might make some impression on the silly youth…. I thought to draw him on more gently by this device." Ralph, it seemed, was a money-lender, and Kate was part of his plan to entrap Lord Frederick.

Kate took time to recover from her ordeal and was with her mother when Ralph arrived with Fanny's letter about Nicholas, which was packed with slanderous exaggerations. Kate cried indignantly, "It is some base conspiracy!" "Everything combines to prove the truth," insisted Ralph.

"A lie!" roared a voice outside. The door was dashed open and Nicholas entered. Furious, he decided he must leave London. Taking his leave of his mother and sister, he told Ralph, "There will be a day of reckoning sooner or later, and it will be a heavy one for you if they are wronged."

Smike and Nicholas travelled to Portsmouth, where they met a certain Mr Vincent Crummles and surprisingly became successful provincial actors.

In London, the bailiffs arrived at Madame Mantalini's shop. In need of new employment, Kate became a companion to the insipid Mrs Witterly in Cadogan Place.

Meanwhile, Lord Frederick and Sir Mulberry hatched a plot regarding Kate. They met Mrs Nickleby at Ralph's office and escorted her home. The attentions of the two noblemen made Kate's life so distressing that she pleaded with her uncle to intervene – to no avail.

*In Victorian times, **companies of actors** would travel from town to town. Before the days of cinema and television, their performances were a popular source of entertainment.*

Newman Noggs overheard Kate's pleas. "Don't cry any more," he whispered, "I shall see you soon. Ha! ha! ha! And so shall somebody else too." He immediately wrote to Nicholas, who set off back to London with Smike.

When Nicholas and Smike stopped for refreshment in a hotel, Nicholas overheard a man referring to "little Kate Nickleby". It was Sir Mulberry out with Lord Frederick. "Your name and address?" demanded Nicholas, keen to defend his sister's honour. When Sir Mulberry refused to give either, Nicholas climbed on to his carriage. Sir Mulberry thrashed Nicholas with his whip, but Nicholas grabbed the handle and sliced his antagonist's face. As the horse bolted, Nicholas was thrown free. Further up the street, the carriage crashed.

Nicholas at once went to Newman, who explained what Kate had been enduring. While Nicholas moved his family from Thames Street, Newman secretly delivered a note from Nicholas to Ralph: "Your kindred renounce you, for they know no shame but the ties of blood which bind them in name with you."

Luckily, Nicholas met Ned and Charles Cheeryble, who employed him as a clerk. One day, Nicholas entered Charles's room to find the pretty girl from the General Agency Office on her knees and in distress. Shocked, he retreated.

Just as things were going better for Nicholas and his family and friends, Smike was captured by Squeers, who locked him in a room at Mr Snawley's house. Only thanks to John Browdie, who was visiting London with his new wife Matilda, was Smike rescued.

Out collecting interest payments from those to whom he had lent money, Ralph met a poverty-stricken man. Twenty years ago this man, Brooker, used to be his clerk, but Ralph treated him badly and they fell out. "Are those of your name dear to you?" Brooker asked threateningly, when Ralph refused to give him money. "They are not," was Ralph's reply.

John and Matilda were taking tea with Mrs Nickleby when Ralph entered with Squeers and Mr Snawley. "I have his father here," claimed Ralph, pointing to Smike. "I want my son," demanded Mr Snawley. Terrified, Smike cried, "I will not go from you with him." Official-looking papers were produced, but Nicholas suspected a cunning trick and Smike stayed.

One day, Charles Cheeryble asked Nicholas if he would help him assist the young woman from the General Agency Office without her father knowing. The young woman was called Madeline Bray and was the daughter of a woman, now dead, whom Charles had loved in his youth. Nicholas agreed.

Meanwhile, Newman Noggs overheard another money-lender, named Gride, telling Ralph about his plans to marry Madeline in return for cancelling a debt. Because Mr Bray was also in debt to Ralph, Gride needed Ralph's help. Newman told Nicholas what he had heard, and the young man pleaded with Madeline not to go ahead with the wedding – to no avail. He even offered Gride money but was refused.

On the morning of the wedding, Nicholas went to the Brays' house with Kate. While he was arguing with Gride and Ralph, the thud of something falling was heard above. Madeline screamed. Her father had dropped dead. Though Gride and Ralph protested, Nicholas carried Madeline to a carriage and took her to stay with his mother.

Gride's housekeeper, the deaf Mrs Sliderskew, soon went missing with some important papers. Squeers was persuaded by Ralph to assist in their recovery. After a clever surveillance operation, Newman Noggs and the Cheeryble brothers' nephew Frank apprehended Squeers and Mrs Sliderskew with the stolen papers. One of the papers found tucked inside Squeers' coat was the will of Madeline Bray's maternal grandfather. Madeline was the beneficiary.

*A **will** is a legal document. It says what a person wants to happen to their property and their money after their death. A **beneficiary** is someone who gains from the will.*

In an effort to restore Smike's failing health, Nicholas took him to Devon. Resting in the garden, Smike was shocked to catch a glimpse of the man who first took him to Dotheboys Hall. Soon afterwards, Smike died.

Things were going from bad to worse for Ralph Nickleby. His associates deserted him, and a bad deal lost him ten thousand pounds. He then learnt from Brooker that, many years ago, when Ralph's estranged wife died, Brooker lied about the fate of Ralph's son. The child did not die but was taken by Brooker to Dotheboys. Said Brooker, "I was confirmed in my design of opening up the secret one day, and making it a means of getting money." Now it was too late – Smike was Ralph's son. As rain and hail pattered against the window, Ralph took his own life.

For others, there was a happier ending. Nicholas married Madeline, and Kate married the Cheeryble brothers' nephew Frank. Mrs Nickleby lived sometimes with her son and sometimes with her daughter. Close to Nicholas lived faithful Newman Noggs.

Up in Yorkshire, "Squeers is in prison, and we are going to run away!" cried a score of shrill voices. Such a cheer rose as the walls of Dotheboys Hall had never heard. As the sound faded, not a boy was left in the school.

Stories from
WILLIAM
SHAKESPEARE

INTRODUCTION

Wiliam Shakespeare, born in Stratford-upon-Avon, England, in 1564, is probably the best-known playwright and poet in the world. Even those who have never seen or read his work unknowingly use Shakespeare's language, for numerous phrases have passed into common use.

The son of a prosperous glover, Shakespeare married Anne Hathaway in 1582 and had three children with her, but it was his move to London that put him on the road to fame and fortune. His plays are enormously varied, including histories, comedies and tragedies. As well as entertaining playgoers for hundreds of years, his works have inspired art, music, literature and films.

Summaries of Shakespeare's plays cannot hope to capture the brilliance of the originals, but it is hoped that the six plays outlined here may encourage readers to look at the complete texts or, better still, to see them performed.

A
MIDSUMMER
NIGHT'S DREAM

Theseus, Duke of Athens, first met his bride-to-be on the field of battle, but thoughts of war soon turned to those of love. She is Hippolyta, Queen of the Amazons, and soon the noble couple will be married with much ceremony.

But elsewhere in the city, true love does not run as smoothly. Egeus, a troubled father, arrives at Theseus' court with his daughter Hermia and two young men, Demetrius and Lysander, in tow. It seems that both are in love with Hermia. Although Egeus favours Demetrius, Hermia has set her heart on Lysander and refuses to obey her father.

Egeus seems prepared to use desperate measures.

I beg the ancient privilege of Athens,
As she is mine, I may dispose of her;
Which shall be either to this gentleman
Or to her death, according to our law…

Hermia appeals to the duke, who confirms that she must obey her father or die – unless she would prefer to live as a nun for the rest of her life. Demetrius, too, tries to persuade her to do her duty. Lysander, naturally, takes a different view!

You have her father's love, Demetrius,
Let me have Hermia's; do you marry him.

Lysander also points out that Demetrius has won the heart of another young woman, a friend of Hermia's called Helena. Theseus admits that he has heard as much and would like to have a word with Demetrius about it. While discussions are taking place, Lysander and Hermia are left alone. Lysander has a plan.

Steal forth thy father's house tomorrow night;
And in the wood, a league without the town…
There will I stay for thee.

A league *was a distance of about three miles. In Elizabethan England, aristocrats loved to hunt for sport and to show off their horsemanship. The wood is also seen as a wild place where anything might happen.*

Hermia is happily agreeing when Helena comes in. The fact that Demetrius prefers Hermia to her is straining the girls' friendship. To reassure Helena, Hermia tells her of her plan to run away. Later, by herself, Helena decides to pass this information on to Demetrius. Maybe it will make him pay attention to her again.

Meanwhile, in a little house in Athens, some workmen have met to plan the entertainment they will put on during the celebrations for the duke's wedding. They are Quince the carpenter, Snug the joiner, Bottom the weaver, Flute the bellows-mender, Snout the tinker and Starveling the tailor.

The friends have decided on an ambitious presentation of *The Most Lamentable Comedy and Most Cruel Death of Pyramus and Thisbe*, a play involving high drama … and a lion! Bottom the weaver is particularly enthusiastic, wanting to play all the parts himself, but in the end he is content to be the hero, Pyramus. It is agreed that the players will all meet in the wood outside the city for secret rehearsals.

It seems that the wood is likely to be a busy place by night! It is already inhabited by a host of fairies, ruled over by Oberon the fairy king and Titania the fairy queen. Also among them is Puck, known as Robin Goodfellow. He is a mischievous sprite who likes nothing better than casting spells and causing trouble.

The humans of Athens are not the only ones to have problems. As Puck tells a passing fairy, Oberon and Titania have quarrelled.

…Oberon is passing fell and wrath,
Because that she as her attendant hath
A lovely boy stolen from an Indian king.
She never had so sweet a changeling;
And jealous Oberon would have the child
Knight of his train, to trace the forest wild;
But she perforce withholds the loved boy,
Crowns him with flowers, and makes him all her joy;
And now they never meet in grove or green,
By fountain clear, or spangled starlight sheen,
But they do square, that all their elves for fear
Creep into acorn cups and hide them there.

Oberon has plans to punish Titania for keeping the boy. He tells Puck to find a certain magical flower. When juice from it is squeezed on a person's eyelids, he or she falls in love with the next creature to appear. If Titania is spellbound in this way, she will not think twice about giving up the boy.

As night falls, Demetrius enters the wood. He is far from happy that Helena insists on following him. "I love thee not, therefore pursue me not," he tells her. Helena will not listen. "I am sick when I do look on thee," says Demetrius, doing his best to shake her off. They do not realize that Oberon is watching and listening.

When Puck returns with the magical flower, Oberon tells him exactly what he plans.

> *I know a bank where the wild thyme blows,*
> *Where oxlips and the nodding violet grows,*
> *Quite over-canopied with luscious woodbine,*
> *With sweet musk-roses and with eglantine.*
> *There sleeps Titania sometimes of the night…*
> *And with the juice of this I'll streak her eyes…*

But Oberon also tells Puck to take some of the juice and put it on Demetrius' eyes, so that he will fall in love with Helena after all.

Oberon finds Titania, surrounded by her sleeping attendant fairies, just as he has planned. Puck, however, not expecting to find many young Athenians wandering around the woods at night, makes a big mistake. He finds Hermia and her lover asleep beneath the trees and puts the juice on Lysander's eyes.

Unfortunately, Lysander awakes when Demetrius comes rushing
past in his attempt to lose his persistent follower. The first person
Lysander sees is not Hermia but Helena! At once, Lysander begins
to vow his love for her. He does not mince his words:

> Content with Hermia! No; I do repent
> The tedious minutes I with her have spent.
> Not Hermia but Helena I love.
> Who will not change a raven for a dove?

Women were not
allowed to act on the
Elizabethan stage.
Female parts were
played by men, which
may have added to the
comedy of some scenes.

Helena, feeling that this is cruel mockery of her unloved state,
runs off, but Lysander follows her, leaving Hermia to sleep on.
When Hermia wakes shortly afterwards, she finds herself alone in
the darkness.

As luck would have it, the Athenian workmen have chosen to hold their rehearsal next to the place where Titania is sleeping. It is soon clear that they have no idea at all about how to stage a play. In addition to the parts already allocated, they decide that it will be necessary for one of them to pretend to be the moon and another to take on the role of a wall.

As usual, Bottom is full of ideas, but when he disappears behind a bush between speeches, Puck sees his chance. He casts a spell over the weaver to give him the head of a donkey! When Bottom reappears, his fellow workmen run away in horror.

Titania, opening her eyes a few moments later, hears Bottom's hearty tones, as he sings to reassure himself. "What angel wakes me from my flowery bed?" she cries, and she falls immediately head-over-heels in love with the extraordinary creature. Titania summons four fairies, Peaseblossom, Cobweb, Moth and Mustardseed to attend on her beloved.

Be kind and courteous to this gentleman.
Hop in his walks and gambol in his eyes;
Feed him with apricocks and dewberries,
With purple grapes, green figs, and mulberries…
And pluck the wings from painted butterflies
To fan the moonbeams from his sleeping eyes.

Of course, Oberon is delighted when he hears what has happened, but his pleasure turns to annoyance when Demetrius hurries past, pursued by Hermia begging for news of Lysander. Oberon realizes at once that Puck has made a mistake and sends him off to find Helena, so that things can be put right. Meanwhile, Demetrius falls asleep in the glade. Oberon seizes the opportunity to squeeze some of the magic juice on his eyes.

No sooner has Demetrius closed his eyes than Lysander and Helena arrive at the same spot. Lysander is giving Helena the benefit of his most poetic speeches. But these are nothing to the flowery outpourings of Demetrius, who wakes to see Helena. "O Helen, goddess, nymph, perfect, divine!" he cries. Helena is close to tears. She is sure she is being made fun of by both men. First no one wanted her, now everyone does! "If you were civil and knew courtesy, you would not do me thus much injury," she says.

At this interesting moment, Hermia stumbles upon her friends, only to find that neither Lysander nor Demetrius pays her the slightest attention. Even Helena is not friendly. She thinks that Hermia helped to plan the trick the men are playing on her. Soon the girls are trading insults among the trees.

Oberon blames Puck for the whole sorry mess. He orders him to split the lovers up so that there is a chance of putting everything right again. Eventually, all four, unknown to each other, drop down to sleep in the same clearing. This time Puck squeezes juice on Lysander's eyes.

Meanwhile, Titania is still in love with Bottom.

> *Come, sit thee down upon this flowery bed,*
> *While I thy amiable cheeks do coy,*
> *And stick musk-roses in thy sleek smooth head,*
> *And kiss thy fair large ears, my gentle joy.*

Oberon, watching, decides that Titania's lesson has gone on long enough. With a spell, he sets her free. "My Oberon!" she cries. "What visions have I seen! Methought I was enamoured of an ass!" Puck removes Bottom's extraordinary head as dawn lights the sky.

It is not long before the sound of hunting horns heralds the arrival of Duke Theseus and Hippolyta, accompanied by Egeus and the rest of the court. Egeus is astonished to find his daughter asleep on the ground. It is, after all, the day on which she must decide her fate.

As the lovers awake, it is soon clear that all is now well. Demetrius loves Helena and is loved in return. Lysander and Hermia are as one again. The duke decides to over-rule Egeus and hold a triple wedding.

Demetrius says what all the lovers are thinking.

In ancient Athens women certainly had little say in their futures, but Shakespeare is also reflecting the fact that in Elizabethan England girls were subject to the will of their father – or an even more powerful man.

Are you sure that we're awake? It seems to me
That yet we sleep, we dream.

Only one set of people is still at odds. In Athens, the workmen are mourning Bottom – and their cancelled play. When the weaver walks in, his old self again, they are overjoyed. The show will go on! Bottom has some final words of advice.

…most dear actors, eat no onions nor garlic, for we are to utter sweet breath; and I do not doubt but to hear them say, it is a sweet comedy.

So Duke Theseus and Queen Hippolyta lead the way to the temple, where they are to be married, and Demetrius follows with Helena, Lysander with Hermia.

That evening, the happy couples celebrate in the duke's palace in Athens. They decide that the play of *Pyramus and Thisbe*, performed by Bottom and his friends, will entertain them. Of course, the play is hilarious, although the actors take their roles very seriously. Bottom, playing Pyramus, makes the most of his dramatic death scene:

Thus die I, thus, thus, thus.
Now am I dead,
Now am I fled:
My soul is in the sky:
Tongue, lose thy light!
Moon, take thy flight!
Now die, die, die, die, die.

When the party is over, and all the performers have gone, the night is left to the fairies. Titania and Oberon wish all the couples well. At last, only Puck is left. He says goodnight to the audience and reminds them that what they have seen is no more real … than a dream.

Hamlet, Prince of Denmark

Something is rotten in the state of Denmark. At midnight, in front of the royal Danish castle of Elsinore, Horatio has come to find out if reports of strange happenings are true. He does not have long to wait. A ghostly figure appears, resembling King Hamlet, who has recently died. At the crowing of a cock, the ghost disappears, but all who see it fear there is trouble to come.

Events have moved fast in the Danish court. Not only has the old king's brother Claudius become king, he has also married his brother's widow, Gertrude. Meanwhile, Fortinbras of Norway is threatening to invade.

In this turbulent setting, one figure is more uneasy than any. It is young Hamlet, son of the former king. His mother begs him to put on a happier face.

Good Hamlet, cast thy nighted colour off...
Thou know'st 'tis common; all that lives must die...

Prince Hamlet wishes to return to his studies in Wittenburg, but both his mother and his stepfather beg him to stay. The young man reluctantly agrees, but when he is alone once more, his words show the full depths of his grief.

> *O, that this too too solid flesh would melt,*
> *Thaw, and resolve itself into a dew!*
> *Or that the Everlasting had not fix'd*
> *His canon 'gainst self-slaughter! O God! God!*
> *How weary, stale, flat, and unprofitable,*
> *Seem to me all the uses of this world!*

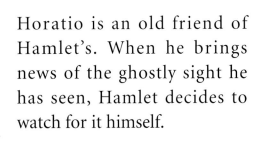

Horatio is an old friend of Hamlet's. When he brings news of the ghostly sight he has seen, Hamlet decides to watch for it himself.

Meanwhile, Laertes, the son of Lord Chamberlain Polonius, is about to return to France. He takes his leave of his sister Ophelia, telling her not to trust too much in the attention that Prince Hamlet has been paying her. Polonius has many final words of wisdom for his son, finishing, at last, by saying:

> *This above all: to thine own self be true,*
> *And it must follow, as the night the day,*
> *Thou canst not then be false to any man.*

Later, while the sound of merrymaking from the palace echoes through the night air, Hamlet and Horatio wait in the biting cold. The ghost appears, beckoning to Hamlet and seeming to wish to speak to him alone.

Hamlet follows the ghost and soon finds his suspicions confirmed. The ghost says that he has been killed by his own brother and asks the prince to revenge this "murder most foul". Hamlet's feelings are in turmoil. His hatred for his uncle makes his mother's actions seem even worse.

O most pernicious woman!
O villain, villain, smiling, damned villain!
…one may smile and smile, and be a villain,
At least I'm sure it may be so in Denmark.

Hamlet swears Horatio to secrecy, but his mind is still racing.

There are more things in heaven and earth,
*   Horatio,*
Than are dreamt of in your philosophy.
…The time is out of joint; O cursed spite…
That ever I was born to set it right!

It is not long before Hamlet's turmoil becomes known to others. Ophelia tells her father of one encounter.

My lord, as I was sewing in my closet,
Lord Hamlet, with his doublet all unbrac'd,
No hat upon his head, his stockings fouled,
Ungarter'd, and down-gyved to his ankle,
Pale as his shirt, his knees knocking each other,
And with a look so piteous in purport
As if he had been loosed out of hell
To speak of horrors, – he comes before me.

A doublet was a short, close-fitting jacket worn by men above a pair of stockings called hose. A full shirt was worn beneath the doublet, which might or might not have sleeves.

Polonius, disturbed by this news, and fearing that it shows Hamlet's passion for Ophelia is verging on madness, hurries to tell the king.

Claudius, however, is already aware of Hamlet's state of mind and suspects he knows its cause. Polonius is typically long-winded in his speech. When at last he explains about Hamlet's behaviour to Ophelia, both the king and the queen are eager to believe this may reveal the cause of Hamlet's erratic behaviour. Polonius suggests that he should eavesdrop on a conversation between the two young people.

No sooner is the plot laid than Hamlet himself appears, reading a book. His replies to questions are ambiguous. Is he really mad or toying with them all? As Polonius says, "Though this be madness, yet there is method in't."

Claudius also tries to find out more by sending two schoolfriends of Hamlet's, Rosencrantz and Guildenstern, to talk with him. Once again, Hamlet appears to be mocking them, but facets of his own dilemma shine through the word-play. "There is nothing either good or bad, but thinking makes it so," he says.

Hamlet makes it clear that he knows why Rosencrantz and Guildenstern are questioning him. He realizes that his behaviour has been causing concern. When the visitors mention that a troop of players has arrived, Hamlet's interest is caught. He welcomes the actors and privately arranges a special performance of a particular play the following night, into which he will add a speech of his own. Later, on his own, Hamlet agonizes over his lack of action and talks of his plan.

> *I'll have these players*
> *Play something like the murder of my father*
> *Before mine uncle, I'll observe his looks…*
> *…the play's the thing*
> *Wherein I'll catch the conscience of the King.*

*A **soliloquy** is a speech spoken by a character on his or her own. Hamlet has many famous soliloquies, which show us what the character is thinking and feeling.*

Polonius' own plan to eavesdrop on Ophelia's next meeting with Hamlet is soon underway. Claudius and Polonius hide as Hamlet approaches. The prince is once again tortured by the situation in which he finds himself.

> *To be, or not to be: that is the question:*
> *Whether 'tis nobler in the mind to suffer*
> *The slings and arrows of outrageous fortune,*
> *Or to take arms against a sea of troubles,*
> *And by opposing end them. To die, to sleep –*
> *No more; and by a sleep to say we end*
> *The heart-ache and the thousand natural shocks*
> *That flesh is heir to; 'tis a consummation*
> *Devoutly to be wished.*

Ophelia's meeting with the prince causes her confusion and distress. One moment he is telling her, "I did love you once." Seconds later, he asserts, "I loved you not." He leaves her feeling wretched and more worried than ever about his state of mind.

> *O, what a noble mind is here o'er-thrown!*
> *The courtier's, soldier's, scholar's, eye, tongue,*
> *   sword;*
> *Th' expectancy and rose of the fair state,*
> *The glass of fashion and the mould of form,*
> *The observ'd of all observers, quite quite down!*
> *And I, of ladies most deject and wretched,*
> *That suck'd the honey of his music vows,*
> *Now see that noble and most sovereign reason,*
> *Like sweet bells jangled out of time and harsh.*

The king, however, is not at all sure that Hamlet is mad. Having overheard everything, he feels alarmed about his own position, and decides to send Hamlet to England.

That night, the theatrical performance that Hamlet has planned with the players is presented before the court. No one who watches can be in any doubt that the subject of the play hits very close to home. A poisoner kills a king and then marries his wife. Claudius rises and stops the show, confirming once and for all in Hamlet's mind that the ghost of his father told the truth.

An arras was a tapestry covering a wall or an alcove. In Elizabethan times, wealthy homes had tapestries for warmth and decoration.

While the king is instructing Rosencrantz and Guildenstern to take Prince Hamlet to England, Gertrude asks to speak to her son. Old Polonius cannot resist the temptation to hide behind the arras and listen to what is said.

The queen, coming straight to the point, tells her son, "Hamlet, thou hast thy father much offended." She means Claudius, of course, but Hamlet takes it another way. "Mother," he says, "you have my father much offended."

As the argument grows heated, Gertrude becomes frightened. When she calls for help, Hamlet hears a sound behind the arras and stabs at it with his sword. He thinks he has killed Claudius at last, but finds only the body of Polonius.

> *Thou wretched, rash, intruding fool, farewell!*
> *I took thee for thy better…*

Hamlet rages at his mother, bringing her at last to a confession that she has acted wrongly. At the height of this dramatic exchange, the ghost of Hamlet's father appears to him once more, urging him to complete his revenge. Gertrude cannot see the ghost, which makes her even more sure that Hamlet is mad.

Later, the queen tells her husband what has happened. Not only has Hamlet killed Polonius, he has hidden the body and is refusing to say where it is. Now Claudius is sure. Whether he is mad or not, Hamlet is too dangerous to allow to live. The king sends with Rosencrantz and Guildenstern letters to the English court, instructing that Hamlet should be put to death on arrival.

Hamlet has gone from the royal castle, but trouble has not left with him. Ophelia, spurned by Hamlet and with her father dead, has lost her reason. News of these events has reached Laertes, who has returned from France.

Unlike Hamlet, Laertes does not hesitate to seek revenge, but Claudius persuades him that his quarrel is with Hamlet. When news comes that Hamlet's ship to England has been attacked by pirates, certainty about the prince's whereabouts is at an end.

Hard on the heels of a message that Hamlet is back on Danish soil comes the news that Ophelia has drowned herself.

There is a willow grows askant the brook,
That shows his hoar leaves in the glassy stream,
Therewith fantastic garlands did she make
Of crow-flowers, nettles, daisies, and long purples
*   …down her weedy trophies and herself*
Fell in the weeping brook. Her clothes spread wide,
And, mermaid-like, awhile they bore her up…
…Till that her garments, heavy with their drink,
Pull'd the poor wretch from her melodious lay
To muddy death.

Hamlet, unaware of what has taken place, meets up with Horatio and returns to complete his revenge. He comes across two grave-diggers, preparing a new grave. Soon, the royal party also arrives, come to bury Ophelia. Hamlet and Laertes fight but are pulled apart. It is arranged that they will have the opportunity to do battle in a more formal setting in the court.

Unknown to Hamlet, Laertes' rapier is poisoned, and so is the wine on a nearby table. The king is unable to prevent Gertrude from drinking it without giving himself away. Meanwhile, both Laertes and Hamlet are slightly wounded by the poisoned blade. As the queen falls to the ground, Hamlet realizes there is treachery afoot. He strikes at the king, knowing himself to be doomed.

Claudius dies, leaving Hamlet for only a few seconds as the King of Denmark. When the arrival of the Norwegian forces is announced, Hamlet confers the throne on young Fortinbras.

…he has my dying voice … the rest is silence.

Horatio is left to mourn.

> *Goodnight, sweet prince,*
> *And flights of angels sing thee to thy rest!*

But it is Fortinbras, the new king,
who has the final word.

> *Let four captains*
> *Bear Hamlet, like a soldier, to the stage,*
> *For he was likely, had he been put on,*
> *To have prov'd most royal.*

MACBETH

Lightning flashes. Thunder roars. On a desolate heath, three witches plan a fateful meeting with a man called Macbeth. The strange women talk in riddles. "Fair is foul, and foul is fair," they chant.

Meanwhile, in an army camp, King Duncan of Scotland hears news of the battle between his men and the rebel forces of Macdonwald, who has sided with the King of Norway. All has gone well for Scotland, but the victory has been hard won. Duncan hears that no sooner has his general Macbeth killed Macdonwald than the King of Norway has launched a fresh attack, this time with the help of another rebel, the Thane of Cawdor. Macbeth and Banquo, another general, have won the day for Scotland. Duncan orders Cawdor's death and expresses his intention of awarding the rebel's title to Macbeth.

Returning, wounded and exhausted, from the battle, Macbeth and Banquo encounter the three witches. "So foul and fair a day I have not seen," says Macbeth, echoing the witches' earlier words. The women greet Macbeth one by one.

All hail, Macbeth! hail to thee, thane of Glamis!
All hail, Macbeth! hail to thee, thane of Cawdor!
All hail, Macbeth, that shalt be King hereafter!

Macbeth appears strangely shocked by these words, but the witches have words for Banquo, too.

Lesser than Macbeth, and greater.
Not so happy, yet much happier.
Thou shalt get kings, though thou be none.

Before the two battle-weary men can ask questions, the witches disappear, leaving Macbeth and Banquo to wonder about what they have heard. Although Macbeth tries to laugh off the prophecies, he is stunned to receive, only a few moments later, the news that he has been made Thane of Cawdor.

Witches *were still burnt at the stake in Shakespeare's day. It was easy for someone to claim that an elderly woman had put a spell on him. Shakespeare's witches speak strangely but truly.*

Could it be that the third prophecy will also come true? Will it come to pass in any case, or must Macbeth himself do something dreadful to make sure he becomes king? As the hero leaves with Banquo, it seems he has made up his mind.

If chance will have me King,
why, chance may crown me,
Without my stir.

Meanwhile, Duncan is unaware of the turmoil in his general's mind. Speaking of the treacherous former Thane of Cawdor, he says, "There's no art to find the mind's construction in the face. He was a gentleman on whom I built an absolute trust." He does not know that the same might be said of Macbeth!

Duncan greets Macbeth and Banquo warmly and takes the opportunity to announce that his son, Malcolm, will be his heir. Furthermore, the king will spend that very night in Macbeth's castle at Inverness.

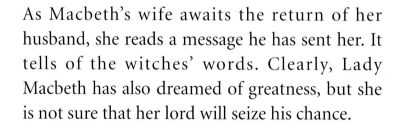

As Macbeth's wife awaits the return of her husband, she reads a message he has sent her. It tells of the witches' words. Clearly, Lady Macbeth has also dreamed of greatness, but she is not sure that her lord will seize his chance.

Yet do I fear thy nature;
It is too full of the milk of human kindness
To catch the nearest way.

When she hears that Duncan will spend the night under her roof, Lady Macbeth is clear that he must never leave the castle alive.

> *…Come, you spirits*
> *That tend on mortal thoughts, unsex me here,*
> *And fill me from the crown to the toe top-full*
> *Of direst cruelty!*

Although Macbeth has ridden on ahead, there is little time for discussion before King Duncan arrives. The King's first words once again underline how unaware he is of the danger he is in.

> *This castle hath a pleasant seat; the air*
> *Nimbly and sweetly recommends itself*
> *Unto our gentle senses.*

Later, as the King dines by torchlight, Macbeth agonizes about the dreadful deed he is considering.

> *He's here in double trust:*
> *First, as I am his kinsman and his subject,*
> *…then, as his host,*
> *Who should against his murderer shut the door,*
> *Not bear the knife myself.*

Lady Macbeth, seeing her husband's indecision, speaks words of shocking violence to urge him to kill the king.

> *I have given suck, and know*
> *How tender 't is to love the babe that milks me;*
> *I would, while it was smiling in my face,*
> *Have pluck'd my nipple from his boneless gums*
> *And dash'd the brains out, had I so sworn as you*
> *Have done to this.*

The couple plan to stab Duncan as he sleeps, then leave the bloody daggers by the king's sleeping servants so that they will take the blame. In the meantime, a smiling host and hostess return to the banquet:

> *False face must hide what the false heart doth know.*

That night, when the King has gone to bed, Macbeth waits for the castle to be quiet. His overwrought imagination plays strange tricks on him.

> *Is this a dagger which I see*
> *before me,*
> *The handle toward my*
> *hand?*
> *Come, let me clutch thee.*
> *I have thee not, and yet I see*
> *thee still.*

Later, Lady Macbeth waits for her husband to come out of Duncan's chamber. She would, she says, have done the deed herself, but the sleeping king reminded her of her father. Macbeth emerges, his hands red with blood. Now it is he who loses his nerve. He does not want to return to the chamber to smear the sleeping servants with blood. Lady Macbeth seizes the daggers and goes in herself.

Just at this moment, the quiet of the castle is shattered by a thunderous knocking at the gates. The porter lets in Macduff and Lennox, who have been asked to rouse the king early so that he can go on his way. It is Macduff who discovers Duncan's body. In the confusion that follows, Macbeth cunningly kills the king's two servants so that they cannot deny the murder. When asked why he did so, he plays his part well.

Who can be wise, amaz'd, temp'rate and furious,
Loyal and neutral, in a moment? No man.

Donalbain and Malcolm, Duncan's sons, realizing that they too may be in danger, decide to flee to Ireland and England.

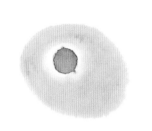

Omens *and portents often feature in Shakespeare's plays. When nature itself seems to mirror the dreadful deeds of men, they appear to be even more significant and, ultimately, tragic.*

To some onlookers, it seems that events outside the castle mirror the unnatural events within. Daylight is overtaken by darkness; wild animals act strangely; and Duncan's horses are said to have attacked each other.

With Duncan's sons gone, Macbeth is the obvious candidate for the throne. Many noblemen, including Banquo, fear that he came by it unlawfully, but now that Macbeth is in power, who dares to challenge him? He publicly blames Duncan's sons for the murder.

Yet Macbeth does not feel secure. In particular, he fears Banquo, who was present when the witches made their prophecy.

To be thus is nothing;
But to be safely thus. Our fears in
Banquo
Stick deep; and in his royalty of nature
Reigns that which would be fear'd.

The king also remembers that it is Banquo's descendants, not his own, who are to be kings. Once again, Macbeth decides there is only one thing to be done. He summons two murderers and orders them to ensure that Banquo never returns from his ride that afternoon.

But even when planning the darkest deeds, Macbeth's inner struggles show on his face. Lady Macbeth speaks firmly.

> *Things without all remedy*
> *Should be without regard; what's done is done...*
> *Gentle my lord, sleek o'er your rugged looks;*
> *Be bright and jovial among your guests tonight.*

Meanwhile, the murderers, joined by a third whom Macbeth has sent to make trebly sure the deed is done, confront Banquo and his son Fleance in open countryside. Banquo is killed, but he is able to warn the boy in time, and Fleance escapes.

That night, Macbeth and his wife host a banquet. Many Scottish lords are there. As the guests take their seats, Macbeth spots one of the murderers at the door. He learns of Banquo's death and Fleance's escape and returns to the feast with a troubled mind.

But when Macbeth reaches the top table, all the places seem to be occupied, although many bid him be seated. To the king's horror, the blood-spattered ghost of Banquo appears to him at the table. This time, Macbeth cannot hide his horror from all present.

Lady Macbeth tries to cover for him.

Sit, worthy friends; my lord is often thus,
And hath been from his youth. Pray you, keep seat;
The fit is momentary; upon a thought
He will again be well.

Indeed, Macbeth does recover his composure when the ghost disappears, but no sooner has he done so than the spectre appears again. Lady Macbeth hurries the guests away, afraid that her husband will say too much in his fearful state. Meanwhile, Macbeth has decided what he must do. He will visit the witches again to find out the worst, for there is no way back now.

I am in blood
Stepp'd in so far that, should I wade no more,
Returning were as tedious as go o'er.

Among the Scottish lords, there is much whispering about the king they now call a tyrant. Many suspect his part in the deaths of Duncan and Banquo. Noble Macduff has gone to the English court to join Malcolm, who is raising an army in order to seize back the throne of Scotland.

In a firelit cavern, Macbeth once more encounters the witches. Once again, Macbeth receives three messages, this time from three apparitions. First, a head in full armour tells him, "Macbeth! Macbeth! beware Macduff…". Then a child covered in blood tells him to be "bloody, bold and resolute … for none of woman born shall harm Macbeth". Finally, the spectre of a child in a crown, holding a tree, gives the news that "Macbeth shall never vanquish'd be until Great Birnam wood to high Dunsinane hill shall come against him".

It seems that Macbeth is safe, but the witches have more to show. An apparition of eight kings followed by Banquo implies that Macbeth's heirs will not reign after him.

Leaving the cave, Macbeth's first thought is to kill Macduff. When he hears that the lord has left for England, he orders that Macduff's wife and children shall be put to the sword instead.

At the English court, news of what has happened to his family fills Macduff and Malcolm with a new fervour to overthrow Macbeth. Edward, King of England, has lent them ten thousand men. They are ready to march on Scotland.

But at the castle of Dunsinane, Lady Macbeth, who once pushed Macbeth towards his fate, has herself broken down under the intolerable strain.

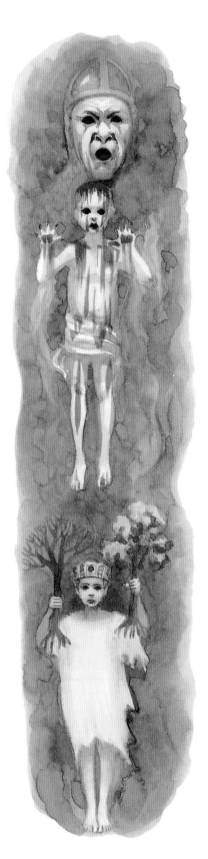

Sleepwalking, she rubs her hands together, as if trying to wash blood from them, and talks wildly of Banquo and Macduff's dead wife. Those listening can no longer be in any doubt about what is on her conscience.

As the English forces approach Birnam Wood, near Dunsinane, Macbeth feels he has nothing to fear.

I'll fight till from my bones
my flesh be hack'd.
Bring me my armour.

Yet news that Lady Macbeth is dead leads Macbeth to face the hopeless bleakness of his life.

Tomorrow, and tomorrow, and tomorrow,
Creeps in this petty pace from day to day
To the last syllable of recorded time;
And all our yesterdays have lighted fools
The way to dusty death. Out, out, brief candle!
Life's but a walking shadow, a poor player
That struts and frets his hour upon the stage
And then is heard no more. It is a tale
Told by an idiot, full of sound and fury,
Signifying nothing.

At this desperate moment, things get worse for Macbeth. A messenger brings the news that Birnam Wood does indeed appear to be moving towards Dunsinane. The soldiers are carrying branches so that their approach and numbers are obscured from the castle. At this moment, we are reminded of Macbeth as he first appeared – a fearless general, leading by example.

> *Blow, wind! come, wrack!*
> *At least we'll die with harness on our back.*

The battle rages with the advantage soon going to the English force, yet Macbeth is determined to fight on. Only when challenged by Macduff does he pause, knowing how much he has already wounded the man. For if Macbeth cannot be slain by a man born of a woman, how can Macduff possibly triumph? Macduff himself has the answer, and it strikes Macbeth like a death blow.

Despair thy charm;
And let the angel whom thou still hast serv'd
Tell thee, Macduff was from his mother's womb
Untimely ripp'd.

Realizing that he has nothing to lose, Macbeth plunges forward.

Lay on, Macduff,
And damn'd be him that first cries,
 "Hold, enough!"

The final moments of Macbeth's life happen offstage. Macduff returns, carrying the head of the tyrant and hails Malcolm as King of Scotland. The tragedy of Macbeth is at an end.

ROMEO AND JULIET

In the Italian city of Verona, two families bear an ancient grudge. In the streets, the servants of the Montague and Capulet families squabble and scuffle. When Benvolio, a nephew to the head of the Montague family, and Tybalt, a nephew to Lady Capulet, come across each other, they are soon using their swords. Only the arrival of Prince Escalus restores the peace. He warns the heads of both families that he cannot tolerate this feud.

> *If ever you disturb our streets again*
> *Your lives shall pay the forfeit of the peace.*

The crowds disperse, leaving the Montagues to talk to Benvolio. Lady Montague asks if Benvolio has seen her son Romeo. It seems he has been acting strangely of late.

As Romeo approaches, Benvolio undertakes to find out what the matter is. It is soon clear that Romeo is in love, but Rosaline, the object of his affections does not return them. Benvolio's advice is matter of fact: "Forget to think of her … examine other beauties."

Meanwhile, the head of the Capulet family is also talking of love. Count Paris, a young nobleman related to Prince Escalus, is eager to marry Capulet's daughter Juliet, who is barely fourteen. Although Capulet would prefer to delay, he tells Paris that Juliet's own feelings will affect his decision. Tonight's feast will give Paris an opportunity to woo Juliet.

High-born ladies in *Shakespeare's time rarely breastfed their children. Often a wet-nurse, who, like Juliet's nurse, had lost her own baby, was used. Juliet's nurse has become almost part of the family.*

In the Capulet house, Lady Capulet decides to have a word with her daughter. Juliet's talkative nurse makes sure she is also present for this most interesting conversation. Lady Capulet comes straight to the point.

> *…think of marriage now; younger than you*
> *Here in Verona, ladies of esteem,*
> *Are made already mothers.*

Juliet shows herself to be an obedient daughter. She promises to look favourably upon Paris but to be guided by her mother.

Outside, Romeo, Benvolio and Romeo's friend Mercutio are preparing to gatecrash the party. As it is a masked ball, they stand some chance of success, but they could be in serious trouble if they are discovered. Romeo feels a sense of foreboding that perhaps is a warning of the tragedy to come.

Inside, all is merriment and dancing. Across the crowded room, Romeo sees a girl who makes all thought of Rosaline fly out of his head and his heart.

> *O, she doth teach the torches to burn bright!*
> *…Did my heart love till now? Forswear it, sight!*
> *For I ne'er saw true beauty till this night.*

It is, of course, Juliet. Unfortunately, Romeo's raptures have drawn the attention of Tybalt, who suspects from his voice that Romeo is a Montague. Tybalt is all for challenging the interloper, but old Capulet, recognizing the man behind the mask, is keen to keep the peace. Tybalt is unhappy, but Romeo meanwhile has taken the opportunity to address Juliet directly. It is not long before she is as smitten as her admirer. As Romeo leaves, Juliet, learning his name at last, realizes how difficult their situation is.

> *My only love sprung from my only hate!*
> *Too early seen unknown, and known too late!*

Later that night, Romeo climbs secretly into the Capulets' orchard. When Juliet appears on her balcony, he is overwhelmed by love for her. Juliet speaks, and her feelings are soon clear:

O Romeo, Romeo! wherefore art thou Romeo?
Deny thy father and refuse thy name;
Or, if you wilt not, be but sworn my
*   love,*
And I'll no longer be a Capulet...
What's in a name?
That which we call a rose
By any other word would smell as
*   sweet...*

Juliet's famous speech *is often misunderstood. "Wherefore" does not mean "where" but "why". Juliet is asking why the man she loves belongs to a rival family.*

Romeo makes himself known to Juliet, and the lovers talk until dawn. If Romeo's intentions are honourable, Juliet says, she will meet him the next day and be secretly married to him. Reluctantly, the lovers part.

Good-night, good-night! Parting is such sweet sorrow...

In the early morning, Friar Lawrence is gathering herbs when Romeo greets him. The friar guesses that Romeo has been up all night. When he hears that Juliet, not Rosaline, is now Romeo's love, the friar sees a chance to end the feud between the Capulets and the Montagues once and for all.

In the streets of Verona, Mercutio and Benvolio are still looking for their missing friend. Tybalt has sent a formal challenge to Romeo's house.

When Romeo turns up at last, the friends engage in joking banter until they come across Juliet's nurse with her servant. It seems she has a message for Romeo. Amid the high-spirited young men, the nurse gives as good as she gets, and she warns Romeo not to trifle with her charge's affections. But in her heart, the nurse is on the side of young love. She promises to tell Juliet to be at Friar Lawrence's cell that afternoon, where she and Romeo can be married.

In the orchard of her father's house, Juliet waits impatiently for the nurse to return. When the good woman arrives, she teases Juliet by holding back her news. At last, however, all is clear. The marriage will go ahead.

It is a hot day. In the streets of Verona, Mercutio and Benvolio unfortunately come across Tybalt and others of the Capulet camp. As insults are exchanged, the arrival of Romeo, already secretly married to Juliet, heats the situation further. Tybalt does not beat about the bush:

Romeo, the love I bear thee can afford
No better term than this: thou art a villain.

Romeo's soft answers to insults exasperate Mercutio, however. He draws his sword, and Tybalt does the same. In vain, Romeo tries to stop them, but his efforts only succeed in hindering Mercutio. With Romeo in the way, Mercutio receives a fatal wound.

With the death of his friend, Romeo runs out of choices. He fights with Tybalt and kills him. Now, under the Prince's edict, Romeo is under a death sentence. He flees as the discovery of Tybalt's bloody body is made.

Although Benvolio speaks up for Romeo when Prince Escalus and the heads of the Montague and Capulet families gather, the prince has had enough of civil strife.

…Let Romeo hence in haste,
Else, when he's found, that hour is his last.

By evening, Juliet, unaware of the events of the afternoon, is eager for the arrival of Romeo. The nurse's news of Tybalt's death leaves the girl in a whirl of emotions. She was fond of Tybalt, but her loyalty to her new husband is stronger. The thought that Romeo has been banished by the Prince is dreadful to her.

Meanwhile, Romeo has sought refuge at Friar Lawrence's cell. Juliet's nurse, finding him there, sees that he is just as distraught as her young mistress. Friar Lawrence tells Romeo to go to Juliet but to leave before dawn for Mantua. In the young man's absence, news of the marriage can be made known and, perhaps, all can be reconciled before his return.

Yet even while the young lovers are secretly meeting in Juliet's chamber, Old Capulet and his wife are planning her marriage to Paris. It is fixed to take place in three days' time.

As dawn draws near, Romeo and Juliet prepare to part on Juliet's balcony. For Juliet the time has come too soon.

Wilt thou be gone? It is not yet near day:
It was the nightingale, and not the lark,
That pierc'd the fearful hollow of thine ear;
Nightly she sings on yond pomegranate-tree.
Believe me, love, it was the nightingale.

The arrival of the nurse, with news that Juliet's mother is on her way, makes the parting more urgent. When Juliet hears that her marriage to Paris has been arranged, she resolutely refuses. Her father arrives to give his weight to the argument, but Juliet's refusal angers him greatly. In the end, he tells his daughter that she will marry Paris or be cast out of her home and family for ever. All Juliet can think of is to consult Friar Lawrence, but already she is considering more desperate measures.

The good friar sees a possible way forward.

> *…go home, be merry, give consent*
> *To marry Paris…To-morrow night…*
> *Take thou this vial, being then in bed,*
> *And this distilling liquor drink thou off;*
> *When presently through all thy veins shall run*
> *A cold and drowsy humour: for no pulse*
> *Shall keep his native progress, but surcease;*
> *No warmth, no breath, shall testify thou livest…*

Thinking she is dead, Juliet's parents will place her in the family vault. Meanwhile, Friar Lawrence will summon Romeo, who will take her back to Mantua. Juliet eagerly agrees to the plan.

In the Capulet house, all is hustle and bustle for the wedding. Juliet's parents are delighted by her apparent change of mind. Once again, no one has any idea of what is going on in Juliet's room. When the nurse goes to wake her in the morning, she finds her charge lifeless on the bed.

Great is the grief in the Capulet household, although Friar Lawrence, knowing more, tries to calm the family. Juliet is carried to the Capulet tomb.

In Mantua, Romeo hears news of Juliet's death before the message from Friar Lawrence reaches him. He feels that there is no point in living. Buying a dram of poison, he sets off for Juliet's grave.

As soon as he hears his message has not arrived, Friar Lawrence, too, hurries to Juliet's tomb, to release her when she awakes.

It is night when Romeo arrives at his beloved's resting place. Unfortunately, Paris has also chosen this moment to pay his respects. Both men are distraught. They fight, and Paris is killed.

Inside the tomb, Romeo kisses Juliet one last time and drinks the poison he has brought. Friar Lawrence arrives too late. As he looks into the tomb, Juliet awakes at last to see the corpses of Paris, Romeo and her kinsman Tybalt, who has been placed in the family tomb, all lying nearby.

At the sound of someone approaching, however, the friar flees, urging Juliet to follow him. But Juliet wants nothing more from life. Seizing Romeo's dagger, she stabs herself and falls beside him.

Summoned by the watchmen, Prince Escalus is first upon the tragic scene, closely followed by the Capulets and the Montagues. The two families are reconciled at last – but at an enormous price.

...never was a story of more woe
Than this of Juliet and her Romeo.

TWELFTH NIGHT

Orsino, Duke of Illyria, is in love, and everyone in the court knows that the lady Olivia is the object of his affections, as he waits for news from her.

If music be the food of love, play on!
Give me excess of it…

Unfortunately, Olivia has recently lost her brother and has vowed not to show her face to the world for seven years. The duke, however, seems determined to wallow in his hopeless passion.

Meanwhile, on the coast of Illyria, a sea captain and some of his crew help a young woman called Viola to the shore. They have all been shipwrecked. Viola's greatest concern is for her brother Sebastian, who is missing and feared drowned.

The captain knows Illyria well and tells Viola about the country. Even he has heard of Orsino's feelings for Olivia! Viola is anxious not to present herself to the world until she feels ready. She asks the captain to help her disguise herself as a boy so that she can seek employment at the duke's court.

In the lady Olivia's house, all is not as sober as might be expected. Her uncle, Sir Toby Belch, and his dim-witted friend, Sir Andrew Aguecheek, are in residence, exasperating and amusing Maria, Olivia's maidservant. Sir Toby, looking for a comfortable life, is hoping that his friend might marry his niece – and meanwhile making free with Sir Andrew's cash.

In the court of Duke Orsino, Viola has found employment and favour. She calls herself Cesario. It is not long before Orsino is asking Cesario to carry messages to Olivia. However, matters are infinitely more complicated than he knows. Not only is Cesario really a woman, but she is also in love with her employer!

A fool, also known as a clown, was often kept in a wealthy household to entertain and amuse. In Shakespeare's plays, fools often speak truths in the form of jokes and riddles.

Viola arrives at Olivia's household, where the lady's fool, Feste, has been entertaining her with witty conversation. Malvolio, Olivia's steward, is less than impressed by this, but his lack of humour does not find favour with Olivia. "O, you are sick of self-love, Malvolio," she says.

Reports of Viola's persistence eventually intrigue Olivia, who veils herself and bids the young man speak. Viola (dressed as Cesario) displays a mixture of intelligence, sympathy and wit that engages the lady far more than Orsino's overblown professions of love have ever done.

When Viola at last sees Olivia's face, she is also seeing the face of her rival.

> *'Tis beauty truly blent, whose red and white*
> *Nature's own sweet and cunning hand laid on.*
> *Lady, you are the cruell'st she alive,*
> *If you will lead these graces to the grave*
> *And leave the world no copy.*

Olivia still wants to hear no more of the Duke, but she already feels more than an interest in Cesario.

> *Get you to your lord.*
> *I cannot love him. Let him send no more, –*
> *Unless, perchance, you come to me again*
> *To tell me how he takes it.*

When Viola leaves, Olivia sends Malvolio after her with a ring, on the pretence that the messenger has dropped it. Viola at once guesses what this means.

> *My master loves her dearly;*
> *And I, poor monster, fond as much on him;*
> *And she, mistaken, seems to dote on me.*
> *What will become of this?*

At this complicated point, we learn that Sebastian, Viola's twin brother, has also escaped death and is on his way to Orsino's court. With him is Antonio, despite the fact that this loyal friend has reason to fear enemies he has made at the court.

Disguises *obviously delighted Shakespeare and his audiences. It was, perhaps, easier than it is today for Sebastian and Viola to seem like twins on the Elizabethan stage, as both of them were played by men!*

That night, Sir Toby and his cronies drink and sing at Olivia's home. Malvolio comes to remonstrate with them.

> *Sir Toby … My lady bid me tell you … If you can*
> *separate yourself and your misdemeanours, you are*
> *welcome to the house; if not, an it would please you to take*
> *leave of her, she is very willing to bid you farewell.*

The revellers are disgusted by Malvolio's pomposity and at once begin to plan how to bring about the steward's downfall. They decide to leave letters around for him to find, hinting that the lady Olivia is in love with him.

Orsino is also up late, sighing and talking of love with the youth he knows as Cesario. When Viola protests that women feel such emotions as strongly as men, she is forced to speak in riddles:

> *My father had a daughter lov'd a man,*
> *As it might be, perhaps, were I a woman,*
> *I should your lordship…*
> *She never told her love,*
> *But let concealment, like a worm i' the bud,*
> *Feed on her damask cheek. She pin'd in thought,*
> *And with a green and yellow melancholy*
> *She sat, like Patience on a monument,*
> *Smiling at grief.*

Moved, but not really knowing why, Orsino gives Viola a jewel to take to Olivia.

At Olivia's house, the plot to ensnare Malvolio is well underway. Maria has faked Olivia's handwriting in a letter full of mysterious hints that she is in love. Of couse, Malvolio is quick to see himself as the cause of her feelings. In particular the letter mentions certain yellow stockings and a wish to see them "ever cross-gartered", as well as advising the reader to "be opposite with a kinsman, surly with servants".

So self-opinionated is Malvolio that he does not notice Olivia's obvious attraction to the messenger from the duke. When Viola calls again, Olivia is frank about her feelings. Viola is as truthful as she can be in the circumstances.

By innocence I swear, and by my youth,
I have one heart, one bosom, and one truth,
And that no woman has; nor never none
Shall mistress be of it, save I alone.

Sir Andrew Aguecheek, for all his foolishness, is more perceptive than Malvolio. "I saw your niece do more favours to the Count's serving-man than ever she bestowed upon me," he tells Sir Toby. Needing Sir Andrew's money, Sir Toby attempts to persuade him that Olivia's actions were merely to inflame the knight further! Sir Andrew decides to write a letter to Cesario, challenging him to a duel.

Nearby, Sebastian and Antonio decide to split up as Antonio does not wish to appear in public in case he is recognized. Sebastian agrees to look after his purse until they meet up that evening.

The astonishing behaviour of Malvolio has come to Olivia's attention. Not only is he wearing yellow stockings with cross-gartering, a fashion she hates, but he is acting very strangely. Only the arrival of Viola draws Olivia's attention away. She tells Sir Toby to take care of Malvolio, convinced that he is losing his mind.

There is also the matter of Sir Andrew's challenge to sort out. The knight words it so mildly that Sir Toby feels Cesario will not take it seriously. He prepares a more robust challenge himself. On receiving the challenge, Viola is horrified. She has no idea how to fight a duel! Sir Toby's tales of Sir Andrew's violent temper unnerve her even more. The trickster Sir Toby meanwhile regales Sir Andrew with news of Cesario's brilliance with the sword. With much trembling on both sides, the two prepare to fight.

It is at this moment that Antonio happens by. He immediately dashes to the aid of the youth he believes to be Sebastian. Before damage can be done, officers arrive and arrest Antonio, but his situation distresses him far less than Viola's refusal to recognize him. She also, of course, denies having his purse.

As Antonio is dragged away, he calls upon his friend Sebastian. Suddenly, Viola is filled with hope that her brother might be alive.

Sebastian, too, finds his identity mistaken, for Feste the fool comes across him, closely followed

by Sir Toby and Sir Andrew. Thinking Sebastian is Cesario, Sir Toby urges them to continue fighting. This time, it is a very different story, and Sir Andrew has much to fear. Luckily, Olivia arrives and breaks up the fight. She leads the astonished Sebastian back to her house, professing her love for him. Sebastian is hardly reluctant. "If it be thus to dream," he says, "still let me sleep!"

Sir Toby's mischief is not yet ended. He has shut Malvolio up in a little, dark room. By the time Sir Toby has finished tricking and goading, even Malvolio believes himself to be mad.

While her varied household is occupied, Olivia is delighted to find that her feelings for Cesario (actually, of course, Sebastian) are returned with passion. Sebastian is only too ready to agree to accompany her to a priest for a secret marriage.

Orsino, arriving in person at Olivia's house, encounters Antonio being brought to the court by the officers. Viola

identifies Antonio as the man who saved her from her duel with Sir Andrew Aguecheek but, of course, continues to deny that she holds his purse.

When Olivia arrives and addresses Cesario/Viola as her lord and husband, confusion reigns, especially when the priest enters and confirms that he has (as he thinks) married the pair. The duke's sense of betrayal is interrupted by the arrival of Sir Andrew, claiming that he and Sir Toby have both been wounded by Cesario. As they are led away to be tended to, the arrival of Sebastian brings about the resolution of the situation.

One face, one voice, one habit, and two persons…

The duke is astonished as he looks from Viola to her brother. Soon, all is clear, and Sebastian and Viola are overjoyed to meet again, while Olivia happily finds her new husband has had no change of heart.

A plaintive letter from Malvolio is delivered to Olivia, showing that he is not mad but badly used. When Malvolio himself is brought forward, the whole trick of the letter is revealed.

Now all that is needed is for Viola to dress again as a woman. All, it seems, will end happily for her as well. Orsino declares:

Cesario, come;
For so you shall be, while you are a man;
But when in other habits you are seen,
Orsino's mistress and his fancy's queen.

As everyone departs, it is left to Feste the fool to end the play with a gently poignant song.

When that I was and a little tiny boy,
  With hey, ho, the wind and the rain,
A foolish thing was but a toy,
  For the rain it raineth every day.

But when I came to man's estate,
  With hey, ho, the wind and the rain,
'Gainst knaves and thieves men shut their gate,
  For the rain it raineth every day.

But when I came, alas! to wive,
  With hey, ho, the wind and the rain,
By swaggering could I never thrive,
  For the rain it raineth every day.

But when I came unto my beds,
  With hey, ho, the wind and the rain,
With toss-pots still had drunken heads,
  For the rain it raineth every day.

A great while ago the world begun,
  With hey, ho, the wind and the rain,
But that's all one, our play is done,
  And we'll strive to please you every day.

ANTONY
AND
CLEOPATRA

In the Egyptian city of Alexandria, all talk is of the love affair between Cleopatra, the queen, and Mark Antony, a Roman general and triumvir. Antony seems to have forgotten his duty and his wife at home. And Cleopatra, a fascinating and beautiful woman, is cleverly doing her best to keep him by her side.

When a messenger brings news that Rome's enemies are gathering and Antony's wife is dead, even the lovesick Roman feels a pang of guilt.

> *I must from this enchanting queen break off:*
> *Ten thousand harms, more than the ills I know,*
> *My idleness doth hatch.*

Cleopatra does her best to make Antony stay, but when she sees that his mind is made up, she wishes him well.

> *…your honour calls you hence;*
> *Therefore be deaf to my unpitied folly,*
> *And all the gods go with you!*

A triumvir *was one of the three men who ruled the Roman empire at this period. They had huge power and responsibilities. The other two triumvirs were Octavius Caesar and Lepidus.*

Meanwhile, back in Rome, Octavius Caesar and Lepidus, Antony's fellow triumvirs, are worried not only by the gossip about Antony but also by the news that Pompey is preparing to attack Rome by sea. Now more than ever they need Antony's brilliance as a general to lead their armies against the enemies of Rome. But will Antony come?

Pompey is concerned to hear that Antony is, in fact, on his way back to Rome. He had hoped not to have to fight against such a great leader. But he comforts himself with the fact that the Romans must be truly worried by his threat if they have to call for Mark Antony.

The meeting of Octavius and Antony is predictably tense, but Antony apologises for his behaviour. Agrippa seizes the opportunity to suggest an even closer bond between the two men. Antony is now a widower, and Octavius has an unmarried sister, Octavia… To calm the situation, Antony agrees to the match.

As Octavius leads Antony off to meet his wife-to-be, Enobarbus, Antony's righthand man, takes the opportunity to catch up with old friends in Rome. Naturally, they are anxious to hear all the latest gossip from Egypt and to find out if Cleopatra is really as amazing as they have heard.

Enobarbus is a soldier, but he becomes a poet as he describes the first time that Antony and Cleopatra met.

The barge she sat in, like a burnish'd throne,
Burn'd on the water: the poop was beaten gold;
Purple the sails, and so perfumed that
The winds were love-sick with them: the oars
*   were silver,*
Which to the tune of flutes kept stroke…

It seems that Cleopatra herself was no less breathtaking.

> *...she did lie*
> *In her pavilion – cloth-of-gold of tissue –*
> *O'er-picturing that Venus where we see*
> *The fancy outwork nature. On each side her*
> *Stood pretty dimpled boys, like smiling Cupids,*
> *With divers-colour'd fans, whose wind did seem*
> *To glow the delicate cheeks which they did cool,*
> *And what they undid did.*

When his friends suggest that Antony must give up Cleopatra now, Enobarbus shakes his head.

> *Never; he will not.*
> *Age cannot wither her, nor custom stale*
> *Her infinite variety.*

Venus *was the Roman goddess of love. In Greek legends, her name was Aphrodite, and her beauty brought about the terrible war of Troy. Cleopatra, too, will be the cause of bloodshed.*

Later, as Antony prepares to leave Caesar's house, he meets an Egyptian soothsayer – a man who claims to see into the future. He warns Antony that Caesar will always triumph in any contest between them.

Although, seconds before, he has promised Octavia that his past behaviour is over, Antony decides to return to Egypt as soon as he can.

Meanwhile, in Egypt, Cleopatra is restless. When a messenger arrives from Rome, she is desperate to hear that Antony is well. The news that he is married is a huge blow, yet within minutes she is plotting how to regain his love.

Near Misenum, the triumvirs meet Pompey to try to avoid the war that threatens. Thanks to Caesar's diplomacy, agreement is reached and a great feast is held on board Pompey's flagship. As the wine flows, the difference in character between sober Caesar and life-loving Antony is all too clear. When Antony leaves for Athens with his new bride in the morning, Octavius is far from sure that her future will be happy.

In Alexandria, Cleopatra finds out details about her rival and feels more confident. "All may be well enough," she tells her maids Iris and Charmian.

The truce between Caesar and Antony does not last long. When, in Athens, Antony hears that Caesar has, after all, waged war on Pompey, he prepares to take up arms against his new brother-in-law. Octavia, torn between the brother she loves and her new husband, begs for the chance to act as go-between. Antony is only too happy to let her go.

As Enobarbus later hears, there is other news from Rome. Octavius has imprisoned Lepidus and taken all the power himself. With Pompey dead, Antony and Octavius are on a collision course, especially as, even before his new wife has reached Rome, Antony is already in Egypt with Cleopatra.

A queen with Cleopatra's qualities would have seemed even more exotic in Shakespeare's England. Elizabeth I, the Virgin Queen, had not long been dead when this play was first performed.

Octavius does not hesitate to tell his sister what has happened. He assures her that the injustice that has been done to her will be revenged.

War is inevitable now, and back in Egypt Cleopatra is determined to play a full part. Enobarbus begs her to withdraw.

> *Your presence needs must puzzle Antony;*
> *Take from his heart, take from his brain, from's time,*
> *What should not then be spar'd.*

But Cleopatra's mind is made up. "I will not stay behind," she says.

News of the approach of Octavius' fleet makes Antony rash. He decides to fight by sea, although his land army is much stronger. Enobarbus, an experienced soldier, begs him to reconsider.

Most worthy sir, you therein throw away
The absolute soldiership you have by land … and
Give yourself merely to chance and hazard,
From firm security.

But Antony will not be advised. All too soon, an appalled Enobarbus hears that the sea battle has been a complete fiasco. It seems that Cleopatra turned her ships for home, and Antony, regardless of the state of the fight, followed her. "I never saw an action of such shame," reports a soldier who was there.

Unsurprisingly, many of Antony's generals and troops also decide to flee – straight to the side of Octavius. Loyal Enobarbus stays with his leader, although everything tells him he is a fool to do so.

It is not long before a full understanding of what he has done catches up with Antony. He begs his remaining friends to make their peace with Rome and hints that there is now only one way open to him. Cleopatra tries to comfort him, explaining that she had no idea he would follow her from the battle. Antony admits that his real conqueror is not Octavius Caesar but his love for the Egyptian queen.

Antony and Cleopatra send messages to Octavius. Antony asks only for his life and to be allowed to live in Egypt, or at least in Athens as a private citizen. Cleopatra asks only that her children can still follow her on the throne. Ceasar's reply is swift:

For Antony,
I have no ears to his request. The Queen
Of audience nor desire shall fail, so she
From Egypt drive her all-disgraced friend,
Or take his life there.

Antony's response is to challenge Octavius to single combat, but even he surely cannot think that the statesman Caesar will risk everything in an unequal battle against a skilled swordsman. Indeed, Caesar has more cunning plans. He sends messengers to try to flatter Cleopatra into betraying Antony.

Antony's misunderstanding of Cleopatra's response to Octavius almost causes a breach between them, but Cleopatra persuades him of her undiminished love and loyalty. Refuelled with courage, Antony determines to fight Caesar to the end.

> *I will be treble-sinewed, hearted, breath'd,*
> *And fight maliciously; … Come,*
> *Let's have one other gaudy night. Call to me*
> *All my sad captains; fill our bowls once more;*
> *Let's mock the midnight bell.*

While Antony and Cleopatra try to act as though all will be well, Octavius is steely and clear-thinking.

> *Let our best heads*
> *Know that to-morrow the last of many battles*
> *We mean to fight.*

As Antony takes his leave of Cleopatra the next morning, both of them know that they may never meet again. Even before the battle, Antony suffers a mighty blow when he hears that Enobarbus has deserted him. Showing his great-heartedness to the last, Antony sends Enobarbus' share of their spoils after him.

The arrival of the treasure from Antony is too much for Enobarbus.

> *I am alone the villain of the earth,*
> *And feel I am so most. O Antony …*
> *I will go seek*
> *Some ditch wherein to die …*

The first day of fighting is by land, where Antony's skill lies. His army is triumphant. In hopeful mood, Antony and Cleopatra celebrate with their generals. But the following day, the collapse of Antony's navy is fast and devastating.

In horror at what he sees and hears, Antony blames Cleopatra, who flees from him in fear for her life. But even at this stage, the queen cannot help scheming to regain Antony's love.

> *To th'monument!*
> *Mardian, go tell him I have*
> *   slain myself;*
> *Say, that the last I spoke was*
> *   "Antony",*
> *And word it, prithee, piteously.*
> *   Hence, Mardian,*
> *And bring me how he takes my*
> *   death.*

Suicide *in the face of dishonour was thought to be a very Roman action. It was considered noble and courageous to take your own life in such circumstances.*

When he is told that Cleopatra is no more, all the fight goes out of Antony.

> *…the long day's task is done,*
> *And we must sleep.*

Thinking of all he has lost, Antony falls upon his sword, but finds himself fatally wounded, not dead. He learns that Cleopatra is still alive and asks to be taken to her.

As Antony dies in her arms, Cleopatra speaks of his greatness.

> *Noblest of men, woo't die?*
> *Hast thou no care of me? Shall I abide*
> *In this dull world, which in thy absence is*
> *No better than a sty? O, see, my women,*
> *The crown o' the earth doth melt. My lord!*
> *O, wither'd is the garland of the war…*
> *And there is nothing left remarkable*
> *Beneath the visiting moon.*

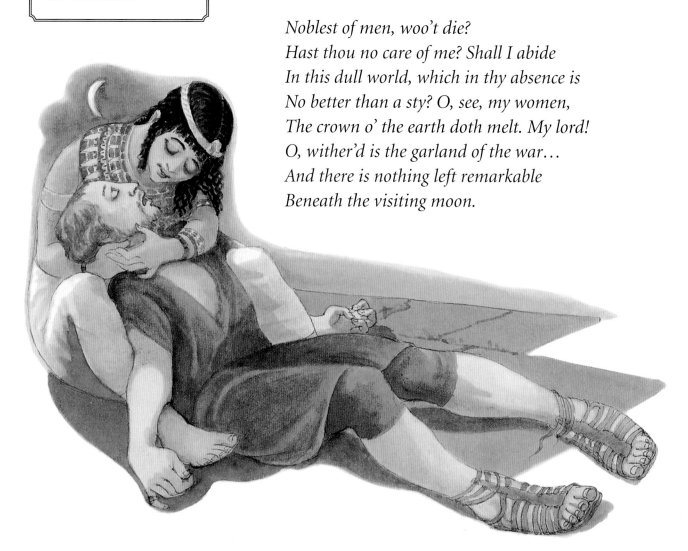

Hearing of Antony's death, even Caesar grieves, but his mind is also on practical matters. He orders that Cleopatra must be guarded to prevent her from following her lover's example.

When Octavius Ceasar comes face to face with Cleopatra, he treats her with respect, but the queen knows that she will be led through the streets of Rome as a captive, when Octavius makes his triumphant return. An asp is smuggled to her in a basket of figs. For Cleopatra, death comes swiftly.

Strangely, it is Caesar, the enemy of Antony and Cleopatra, who ensures that the lovers will be reunited in death.

She shall be buried by her
*   Antony;*
No grave upon the earth shall
*   clip in it*
A pair so famous.

An asp is a small venomous snake, found in North Africa and Arabia. It seems that Cleopatra was ready for this moment, having studied painless and foolproof ways of committing suicide.

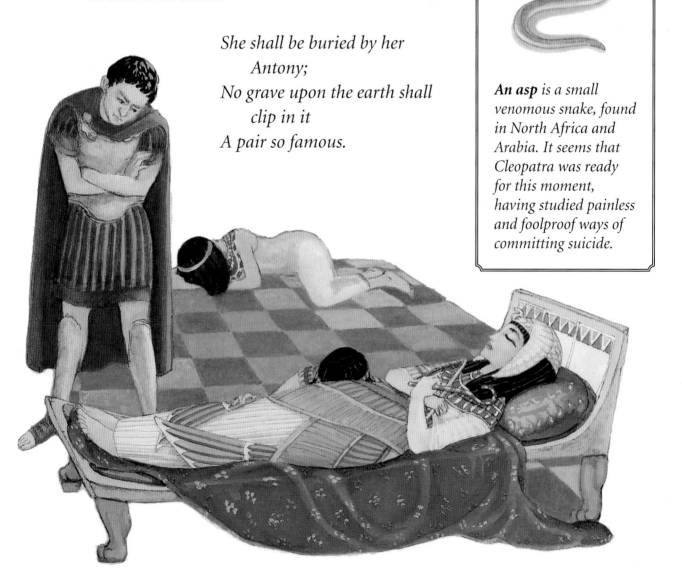

Stories from
OSCAR WILDE

INTRODUCTION

OSCAR WILDE died in Paris in November 1900 but his fame lives on. He is known for his plays, stories and poems, and for the witty and amusing comments he made on a huge range of topics (although Queen Victoria, he said, was not a fit subject). Whether all of these were of his own invention, or borrowed and adapted, is not always clear. "I wish I had said that," he is claimed to have commented when a friend made a clever remark. "You will, Oscar, you will!" came the reply.

Some readers may be surprised that this famous personality also wrote stories for children. His own mother, Jane Francisca Speranza Wilde, was a well known writer too. Perhaps she told stories to her children when they were small, inspiring her son to entertain his own children in turn. Oscar Wilde's stories for children are full of humour, but they do not ignore the sadder, harsher side of life. Their bitter-sweet flavour ensures that they are enjoyed by thoughtful children and adults alike.

THE NIGHTINGALE AND THE ROSE

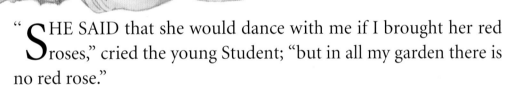

"SHE SAID that she would dance with me if I brought her red roses," cried the young Student; "but in all my garden there is no red rose."

From her nest in the holm-oak tree the Nightingale heard him, and she looked out through the leaves, and wondered.

"No red rose in all my garden!" he cried, and his beautiful eyes filled with tears. "Ah, on what little things does happiness depend! I have read all that the wise men have written, and all the secrets of philosophy are mine, yet for want of a red rose is my life made wretched."

"Here at last is a true lover," said the Nightingale. "Night after night have I sung of him, though I knew him not: night after night have I told his story to the stars, and now I see him. His hair is dark as the hyacinth-blossom, and his lips are red as the rose of his desire; but passion has made his face like pale ivory, and sorrow has set her seal upon his brow."

"The Prince gives a ball to-morrow night," murmured the young Student, "and my love will be of the company. If I bring her a red rose she will dance with me till dawn. If I bring her a red rose, I shall hold her in my arms, and she will lean her head upon my shoulder, and her hand will be clasped in mine. But there is no red rose in my garden, so I shall sit lonely, and she will pass me by. She will have no heed of me, and my heart will break."

"Here indeed is the true lover," said the Nightingale. "What I sing of, he suffers: what is joy to me, to him is pain. Surely Love is a wonderful thing. It is more precious than emeralds, and dearer than fine opals. Pearls and pomegranates cannot buy it, nor is it set forth in the market-place. It may not be purchased of the merchants, nor can it be weighed out in the balance for gold."

"The musicians will sit in their gallery," said the young Student, "and play upon their stringed instruments, and my love will dance to the sound of the harp and the violin. She will dance so lightly that her feet will not touch the floor, and the courtiers in their gay dresses will throng round her. But with me she will not dance, for I have no red rose to give her;" and he flung himself down on the grass, and buried his face in his hands, and wept.

"Why is he weeping?" asked a little Green Lizard, as he ran past him with his tail in the air.

"Why, indeed?" said a Butterfly, who was fluttering about after a sunbeam.

"Why, indeed?" whispered a Daisy to his neighbour, in a soft, low voice.

"He is weeping for a red rose," said the Nightingale.

"For a red rose!" they cried; "how very ridiculous!" and the little Lizard, who was something of a cynic, laughed outright.

But the Nightingale understood the secret of the Student's sorrow, and she sat silent in the oak-tree, and thought about the mystery of Love.

Suddenly she spread her brown wings for flight, and soared into the air. She passed through the grove like a shadow, and like a shadow she sailed across the garden.

In the centre of the grass-plot was standing a beautiful Rose-tree, and when she saw it, she flew over to it, and lit upon a spray.

"Give me a red rose," she cried, "and I will sing you my sweetest song."

But the Tree shook its head.

"My roses are white," it answered; "as white as the foam of the sea, and whiter than the snow upon the mountain. But go to my brother who grows round the old sun-dial, and perhaps he will give you what you want."

So the Nightingale flew over to the Rose-tree that was growing round the old sun-dial.

"Give me a red rose," she cried, "and I will sing you my sweetest song."

But the Tree shook its head.

"My roses are yellow," it answered; "as yellow as the hair of the mermaiden who sits upon an amber throne, and yellower than the daffodil that blooms in the meadow before the mower comes with his scythe. But go to my brother who grows beneath the Student's window, and perhaps he will give you what you want."

So the Nightingale flew over to the Rose-tree that was growing beneath the Student's window.

"Give me a red rose," she cried, "and I will sing you my sweetest song."

But the Tree shook its head.

"My roses are red," it answered, "as red as the feet of the dove, and redder than the great fans of coral that wave and wave in the ocean-cavern. But the winter has chilled my veins, and the frost has nipped my buds, and the storm has broken my branches, and I shall have no roses at all this year."

"One red rose is all I want," cried the Nightingale, "only one red rose! Is there no way by which I can get it?"

"There is a way," answered the Tree; "but it is so terrible that I dare not tell it to you."

"Tell it to me," said the Nightingale, "I am not afraid."

"If you want a red rose," said the Tree, "you must build it out of music by moonlight, and stain it with your own heart's-blood. You must sing to me with your breast against a thorn. All night long you must sing to me, and the thorn must pierce your heart, and your life-blood must flow into my veins, and become mine."

"Death is a great price to pay for a red rose," cried the Nightingale, "and Life is very dear to all. It is pleasant to sit in the green wood, and to watch the Sun in his chariot of gold, and the Moon in her chariot of pearl. Sweet is the scent of the hawthorn, and sweet are the bluebells that hide in the valley, and the heather that blows on the hill. Yet Love is better than Life, and what is the heart of a bird compared to the heart of a man?"

So she spread her brown wings for flight, and soared into the air. She swept over the garden like a shadow, and like a shadow she sailed through the grove.

The young Student was still lying on the grass, where she had left him, and the tears were not yet dry in his beautiful eyes.

"Be happy," cried the Nightingale, "be happy; you shall have your red rose. I will build it out of music by moonlight, and stain it with my own heart's-blood. All that I ask of you in return is that you will be a true lover, for Love is wiser than Philosophy, though she is wise, and mightier than Power, though he is mighty. Flame-coloured are his wings, and coloured like flame is his body. His lips are sweet as honey, and his breath is like frankincense."

 The Student looked up from the grass, and listened, but he could not understand what the Nightingale was saying to him, for he only knew the things that are written down in books.

But the Oak-tree understood, and felt sad, for he was very fond of the little Nightingale who had built her nest in his branches.

"Sing me one last song," he whispered; "I shall feel very lonely when you are gone."

So the Nightingale sang to the Oak-tree, and her voice was like water bubbling from a silver jar.

When she had finished her song the Student got up, and pulled a note-book and a lead-pencil out of his pocket.

"She has form," he said to himself, as he walked away through the grove – "that cannot be denied to her; but has she got feeling? I am afraid not. In fact, she is like most artists; she is all style without any sincerity. She would not sacrifice herself for others. She thinks merely of music, and everybody knows that the arts are selfish. Still, it must be admitted that she has some beautiful notes in her voice. What a pity it is that they do not mean anything, or do any practical good." And he went into his room, and lay down on his little pallet-bed, and began to think of his love; and, after a time, he fell asleep.

And when the Moon shone in the heavens the Nightingale flew to the Rose-tree, and set her breast against the thorn. All night long she sang with her breast against the thorn, and the cold crystal Moon leaned down and listened.

All night long she sang, and the thorn went deeper and deeper into her breast, and her life-blood ebbed away from her.

She sang first of the birth of love in the heart of a boy and a girl. And on the topmost spray of the Rose-tree there blossomed a marvellous rose, petal following petal, as song followed song. Pale was it, at first, as the mist that hangs over the river – pale as the feet of the morning, and silver as the wings of the dawn. As the shadow of a rose in a mirror of silver, as the shadow of a rose in a water-pool, so was the rose that blossomed on the topmost spray of the Tree.

But the Tree cried to the Nightingale to press closer against the thorn. "Press closer, little Nightingale," cried the Tree, "or the Day will come before the rose is finished."

So the Nightingale pressed close against the thorn, and louder and louder grew her song, for she sang of the birth of passion in the soul of a man and a maid.

And a delicate flush of pink came into the leaves of the rose, like the flush in the face of the bridegroom when he kisses the lips of the bride. But the thorn had not yet reached her heart, so the rose's heart remained white, for only a Nightingale's heart's-blood can crimson the heart of a rose.

And the Tree cried to the Nightingale to press closer against the thorn. "Press closer, little Nightingale," cried the Tree, "or the Day will come before the rose is finished."

So the Nightingale pressed closer against the thorn, and the thorn touched her heart, and a fierce pang of pain shot through her. Bitter, bitter was the pain, and wilder and wilder grew her song, for she sang of the Love that is perfected by Death, of the Love that dies not in the tomb.

And the marvellous rose became crimson, like the rose of the eastern sky. Crimson was the girdle of petals, and crimson as a ruby was the heart.

But the Nightingale's voice grew fainter, and her little wings began to beat, and a film came over her eyes. Fainter and fainter grew her song, and she felt something choking her in her throat.

Then she gave one last burst of music. The white Moon heard it, and she forgot the dawn, and lingered on in the sky. The red rose heard it, and it trembled all over with ecstasy, and opened its petals to the cold morning air. Echo bore it to her purple cavern in the hills, and woke the sleeping shepherds from their dreams. It floated through the reeds of the river, and they carried its message to the sea.

"Look, look!" cried the Tree, "the rose is finished now;" but the Nightingale made no answer, for she was lying dead in the long grass, with the thorn in her heart.

And at noon the Student opened his window and looked out.

"Why, what a wonderful piece of luck!" he cried; "here is a red rose! I have never seen any rose like it in all my life. It is so beautiful that I am sure it has a long Latin name;" and he leaned down and plucked it.

Then he put on his hat, and ran up to the Professor's house with the rose in his hand.

The daughter of the Professor was sitting in the doorway winding blue silk on a reel, and her little dog was lying at her feet.

"You said that you would dance with me if I brought you a red rose," cried the Student. "Here is the reddest rose in all the world. You will wear it to-night next your heart, and as we dance together it will tell you how I love you."

But the girl frowned.

"I am afraid it will not go with my dress," she answered; "and, besides, the Chamberlain's nephew has sent me some real jewels, and everybody knows that jewels cost far more than flowers."

"Well, upon my word, you are very ungrateful," said the Student angrily; and he threw the rose into the street, where it fell into the gutter, and a cartwheel went over it.

"Ungrateful!" said the girl. "I tell you what, you are very rude; and, after all, who are you? Only a Student. Why, I don't believe you have even got silver buckles to your shoes as the Chamberlain's nephew has;" and she got up from her chair and went into the house.

"What a silly thing Love is," said the Student as he walked away. "It is not half as useful as Logic, for it does not prove anything, and it is always telling one of things that are not going to happen, and making one believe things that are not true. In fact, it is quite unpractical, and, as in this age to be practical is everything, I shall go back to Philosophy and study Metaphysics."

So he returned to his room and pulled out a great dusty book, and began to read.

THE DEVOTED FRIEND

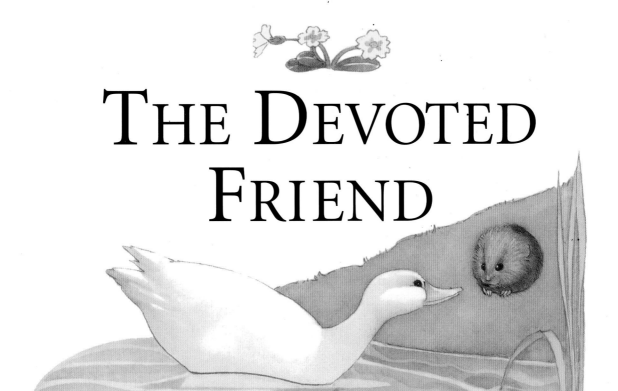

ONE MORNING the old Water-rat put his head out of his hole. He had bright beady eyes and stiff grey whiskers, and his tail was like a long bit of black india-rubber. The little ducks were swimming about in the pond, looking just like a lot of yellow canaries, and their mother, who was pure white with real red legs, was trying to teach them how to stand on their heads in the water.

"You will never be in the best society unless you can stand on your heads," she kept saying to them; and every now and then she showed them how it was done. But the little ducks paid no attention to her. They were so young that they did not know what an advantage it is to be in society at all.

"What disobedient children!" cried the old Water-rat; "they really deserve to be drowned."

"Nothing of the kind," answered the Duck, "every one must make a beginning, and parents cannot be too patient."

"Ah! I know nothing about the feelings of parents," said the Water-rat; "I am not a family man. In fact, I have never been married, and I never intend to be. Love is all very well in its way, but friendship is much higher. Indeed, I know of nothing in the world that is either nobler or rarer than a devoted friendship."

"And what, pray, is your idea of the duties of a devoted friend?" asked a green Linnet, who was sitting in a willow-tree hard by, and had overheard the conversation.

"Yes, that is just what I want to know," said the Duck, and she swam away to the end of the pond, and stood upon her head, in order to give her children a good example.

"What a silly question!" cried the Water-rat. "I should expect my devoted friend to be devoted to me, of course."

"And what would you do in return?" asked the little bird, swinging upon a silver spray, and flapping his tiny wings.

"I don't understand you," answered the Water-rat.

"Let me tell you a story on the subject," said the Linnet.

"Is the story about me?" asked the Water-rat. "If so, I will listen to it, for I am extremely fond of fiction."

"It is applicable to you," answered the Linnet. He flew down, and alighting upon the bank, told the story of The Devoted Friend.

"Once upon a time," said the Linnet, there was an honest little fellow named Hans."

"Was he very distinguished?" asked the Water-rat.

"No," answered the Linnet, "I don't think he was distinguished at all, except for his kind heart, and his funny round good-humoured face. He lived in a tiny cottage all by himself, and every day he worked in his garden. In all the country-side there was no garden so lovely as his. Sweet-william grew there, and Gilly-flowers, and Shepherds'-purses, and Fair-maids of France. There were damask

Roses, and yellow Roses, lilac Crocuses, and gold, purple Violets and white. Columbine and Ladysmock, Marjoram and Wild Basil, the Cowslip and the Flower-de-luce, the Daffodil and the Clove-Pink bloomed or blossomed in their proper order as the months went by, one flower taking another flower's place, so that there were always beautiful things to look at, and pleasant odours to smell.

"Little Hans had a great many friends, but the most devoted friend of all was big Hugh the Miller. Indeed, so devoted was the rich Miller to little Hans, that he would never go by his garden without leaning over the wall and plucking a large nosegay, or a handful of sweet herbs, or filling his pockets with plums and cherries if it was the fruit season.

"'Real friends should have everything in common,' the Miller used to say, and little Hans nodded and smiled, and felt very proud of having a friend with such noble ideas.

"Sometimes, indeed, the neighbours thought it strange that the rich Miller never gave little Hans anything in return, though he had a hundred sacks of flour stored away in his mill, and six milch cows, and a large flock of woolly sheep; but Hans never troubled his head about these things, and nothing gave him greater pleasure than to listen to all the wonderful things the Miller used to say about the unselfishness of true friendship.

"So little Hans worked away in his garden. During the spring, the summer, and the autumn he was very happy, but when the winter came, and he had no fruit or flowers to bring to the market, he suffered a good deal from cold and hunger, and often had to go to bed without any supper but a few dried pears or some hard nuts. In the winter, also, he was extremely lonely, as the Miller never came to see him then.

"'There is no good in my going to see little Hans as long as the snow lasts,' the Miller used to say to his Wife, 'for when people are in trouble they should be left alone, and not be bothered by visitors. That at least is my idea about friendship, and I am sure I am right. So I shall wait till the spring comes, and then I shall pay him a visit, and he will be able to give me a large basket of primroses, and that will make him so happy.'

"'You are certainly very thoughtful about others,' answered the Wife, as she sat in her comfortable armchair by the big pinewood fire; 'very thoughtful indeed. It is quite a treat to hear you talk about friendship. I am sure the clergyman himself could not say such beautiful things as you do, though he does live in a three-storied house, and wear a gold ring on his little finger.'

"'But could we not ask little Hans up here?' said the Miller's youngest son. 'If poor Hans is in trouble I will give him half my porridge, and show him my white rabbits.'

"'What a silly boy you are!' cried the Miller; 'I really don't know what is the use of sending you to school. You seem not to learn anything. Why, if little Hans came up here, and saw our warm fire, and our good supper, and our great cask of red wine, he might get envious, and envy is a most terrible thing, and would spoil anybody's nature. I certainly will not allow Hans's nature to be spoiled. I am his best friend, and I will always watch over him, and see that he is not led into any temptations. Besides, if Hans came here, he might ask me to let him have some flour on credit, and that I could not do. Flour is one thing, and friendship is another, and they should not be confused. Why, the words are spelt differently, and mean quite different things. Everybody can see that.'

"'How well you talk!' said the Miller's Wife, pouring herself out a large glass of warm ale; 'really I feel quite drowsy. It is just like being in church.'

"'Lots of people act well,' answered the Miller; 'but very few people talk well, which shows that talking is much the more difficult thing of the two, and much the finer thing also;' and he looked sternly across the table at his little son, who felt so ashamed of himself that he hung his head down, and grew quite scarlet, and began to cry into his tea. However, he was so young that you must excuse him."

"Is that the end of the story?" asked the Water-rat.

"Certainly not," answered the Linnet, "that is the beginning."

"Then you are quite behind the age," said the Water-rat. "Every good story-teller now-adays starts with the end, and then goes on to the beginning, and concludes with the middle. That is the new method. I heard all about it the other day from a critic who was walking round the pond with a young man. He spoke of the matter at great length, and I am sure he must have been right, for he had blue spectacles and a bald head, and whenever the young man made any remark, he always answered 'Pooh!' But pray go on with your story. I like the Miller immensely. I have all kinds of beautiful sentiments myself, so there is a great sympathy between us."

"Well," said the Linnet, hopping now on one leg and now on the other, "as soon as the winter was over, and the primroses began to open their pale yellow stars, the Miller said to his Wife that he would go down and see little Hans.

"'Why, what a good heart you have!' cried his Wife; 'you

are always thinking of others. And mind you take the big basket with you for the flowers.'

"So the Miller tied the sails of the windmill together with a strong iron chain, and went down the hill with the basket on his arm.

"'Good morning, little Hans,' said the Miller.

"'Good morning,' said Hans, leaning on his spade, and smiling from ear to ear.

"'And how have you been all the winter?' said the Miller.

"'Well, really,' cried Hans, 'it is very good of you to ask, very good indeed. I am afraid I had rather a hard time of it, but now the spring has come, and I am quite happy, and all my flowers are doing well.'

"'We often talked of you during the winter, Hans,' said the Miller, 'and wondered how you were getting on.'

"'That was kind of you,' said Hans; 'I was half afraid you had forgotten me.'

"'Hans, I am surprised at you,' said the Miller; 'friendship never forgets. That is the wonderful thing about it, but I am afraid you don't understand the poetry of life. How lovely your primroses are looking, by-the-bye!'

"'They are certainly very lovely,' said Hans, 'and it is a most lucky thing for me that I have so many. I am going to bring them into the market and sell them to the Burgomaster's daughter, and buy back my wheelbarrow with the money.'

"'Buy back your wheelbarrow? You don't mean to say you have sold it? What a very stupid thing to do!'

"'Well, the fact is,' said Hans, 'that I was obliged to. You see the winter was a very bad time for me, and I really had no money at all to buy bread with. So I first sold the silver buttons off my Sunday coat, and then I sold my silver chain, and then I sold my big pipe, and at last I sold my wheelbarrow. But I am going to buy them all back again now.'

"'Hans,' said the Miller, 'I will give you my wheelbarrow. It is not in very good repair; indeed, one side is gone, and there is something wrong with the wheel-spokes; but in spite of that I will give it to you. I know it is very generous of me, and a great many people would think me extremely foolish for parting with it, but I am not like the rest of the world. I think that generosity is the essence of friendship, and, besides, I have got a new wheel-barrow for myself. Yes, you may set your mind at ease. I will give you my wheelbarrow.'

"'Well, really, that is generous of you,' said little Hans, and his funny round face glowed all over with pleasure. 'I can easily put it in repair, as I have a plank of wood in the house.'

"'A plank of wood!' said the Miller; 'why, that is just what I want for the roof of my barn. There is a very large hole in it, and the corn will all get damp if I don't stop it up. How lucky you mentioned it! It is quite remarkable how one good action always breeds another. I have given you my wheelbarrow, and now you are going to give me your plank. Of course, the wheelbarrow is worth far more than the plank, but true friendship never notices things like that. Pray get it at once, and I will set to work at my barn this very day.'

"'Certainly,' cried little Hans, and he ran into the shed and dragged the plank out."

"'It is not a very big plank,' said the Miller, looking at it, 'and I am afraid that after I have mended my barn-roof there won't be any left for you to mend the wheelbarrow with; but, of course, that is not my fault. And now, as I have given you my wheelbarrow, I am sure you would like to give me some flowers in return. Here is the basket, and mind you fill it quite full.'

"'Quite full?' said little Hans, rather sorrowfully, for it was really a very big basket, and he knew that if he filled it he would have no flowers left for the market, and he was very anxious to get his silver buttons back.

"'Well, really,' answered the Miller, 'as I have given you my wheelbarrow, I don't think that it is much to ask you for a few flowers. I may be wrong, but I should have thought that friendship, true friendship, was quite free from selfishness of any kind.'

'My dear friend, my best friend,' cried little Hans, 'you are welcome to all the flowers in my garden. I would much sooner have your good opinion than my silver buttons, any day;' and he ran and plucked all his pretty primroses, and filled the Miller's basket.

"'Good-bye, little Hans, said the Miller, as he went up the hill with the plank on his shoulder, and the big basket in his hand.

"'Good-bye,' said little Hans, and he began to dig away quite merrily, he was so pleased about the wheelbarrow.

"The next day he was nailing up some honeysuckle against the porch, when he heard the Miller's voice calling to him from the road. So he jumped off the ladder, and ran down the garden, and looked over the wall.

"There was the Miller with a large sack of flour on his back.

"'Dear little Hans,' said the Miller, 'would you mind carrying this sack of flour for me to market?'

"'Oh, I am so sorry,' said Hans, 'but I am really very busy to-day. I have got all my creepers to nail up, and all my flowers to water, and all my grass to roll.'

"'Well, really,' said the Miller, 'I think that, considering that I am going to give you my wheelbarrow, it is rather unfriendly of you to refuse.'

"'Oh, don't say that,' cried little Hans, 'I wouldn't be unfriendly for the whole world;' and he ran in for his cap, and trudged off with the big sack on his shoulders.

"It was a very hot day, and the road was terribly dusty, and before Hans had reached the sixth milestone he was so tired that he had to sit down and rest. However, he went on bravely, and at last he reached the market. After he had waited there some time, he sold the sack of flour for a very good price, and then he returned home at once, for he was afraid that if he stopped too late he might meet some robbers on the way.

"'It has certainly been a hard day,' said little Hans to himself as he was going to bed, 'but I am glad I did not refuse the Miller, for he is my best friend, and, besides, he is going to give me his wheelbarrow.'

"Early the next morning the Miller came down to get the money for his sack of flour, but little Hans was so tired that he was still in bed.

"'Upon my word,' said the Miller, 'you are very lazy. Really, considering that I am going to give you my wheelbarrow, I think you might work harder. Idleness is a great sin, and I certainly don't like any of my friends to be idle or sluggish. You must not mind my speaking quite plainly to you. Of course I should not dream of doing so if I were not your friend. But what is the good of friendship if one cannot say exactly what one means? Anybody can say charming things and try to please and to flatter, but a true friend always says unpleasant things, and does not mind giving pain. Indeed, if he is a really true friend he prefers it, for he knows that then he is doing good.'

"'I am very sorry,' said little Hans, rubbing his eyes and pulling off his night-cap, 'but I was so tired that I thought I would lie in bed for a little time, and listen to the birds singing. Do you know that I always work better after hearing the birds sing?'

"'Well, I am glad of that,' said the Miller, clapping little Hans on the back, 'for I want you to come up to the mill as soon as you are dressed, and mend my barn-roof for me.'

"Poor little Hans was very anxious to go and work in his garden, for his flowers had not been watered for two days, but he did not like to refuse the Miller, as he was such a good friend to him.

"'Do you think it would be unfriendly of me if I said I was busy?' he inquired in a shy and timid voice.

"'Well, really' answered the Miller, 'I do not think it is much to ask of you, considering that I am going to give you my wheelbarrow; but of course if you refuse I will go and do it myself.'

"'Oh! on no account,' cried little Hans; and he jumped out of bed, and dressed himself, and went up to the barn.

"He worked there all day long, till sunset, and at sunset the Miller came to see how he was getting on.

"'Have you mended the hole in the roof yet, little Hans?' cried the Miller in a cheery voice.

"'It is quite mended,' answered little Hans, coming down the ladder.

"'Ah!' said the Miller, 'there is no work so delightful as the work one does for others.'

"'It is certainly a great privilege to hear you talk,' answered little Hans, sitting down and wiping his forehead, 'a very great privilege. But I am afraid I shall never have such beautiful ideas as you have.'

"'Oh! they will come to you,' said the Miller, 'but you must take more pains. At present you have only the practice of friendship; some day you will have the theory also.'

"'Do you really think I shall?' asked little Hans.

"'I have no doubt of it,' answered the Miller, 'but now that you have mended the roof, you had better go home and rest, for I want you to drive my sheep to the mountain tomorrow.

"Poor little Hans was afraid to say anything to this, and early the next morning the Miller brought his sheep round to the cottage, and Hans started off with them to the mountain. It took him the whole day to get there and back; and when he returned he was so tired that he went off to sleep in his chair, and did not wake up till it was broad daylight.

"'What a delightful time I shall have in my garden,' he said, and he went to work at once.

"But somehow he was never able to look after his flowers at all, for his friend the Miller was

always coming round and sending him off on long errands, or getting him to help at the mill. Little Hans was very much distressed at times, as he was afraid his flowers would think he had forgotten them, but he consoled himself by the reflection that the Miller was his best friend. 'Besides,' he used to say, 'he is going to give me his wheelbarrow, and that is an act of pure generosity.'

"So little Hans worked away for the Miller, and the Miller said all kinds of beautiful things about friendship, which Hans took down in a note-book, and used to read over at night, for he was a very good scholar.

"Now it happened that one evening little Hans was sitting by his fireside when a loud rap came at the door. It was a very wild night, and the wind was blowing and roaring round the house so terribly that at first he thought it was merely the storm. But a second rap came, and then a third, louder than either of the others.

"'It is some poor traveller,' said little Hans to himself, and he ran to the door.

"There stood the Miller with a lantern in one hand and a big stick in the other.

"'Dear little Hans,' cried the Miller, 'I am in great trouble. My little boy has fallen off a ladder and hurt himself, and I am going for the Doctor. But he lives so far away, and it is such a bad night, that it has just occurred to me that it would be much better if you went instead of me. You know I am going to give you my wheelbarrow, and so it is only fair that you should do something for me in return.'

"'Certainly,' cried little Hans, 'I take it quite as a compliment your coming to me, and I will start off at once. But you must lend me your lantern, as the night is so dark that I am afraid I might fall into the ditch.'

"'I am very sorry,' answered the Miller, 'but it is my new lantern, and it would be a great loss to me if anything happened to it.'

"'Well, never mind, I will do without it,' cried little Hans, and he took down his great fur coat, and his warm scarlet cap, and tied a muffler round his throat, and started off.

"What a dreadful storm it was! The night was so black that little Hans could hardly see, and the wind was so strong that he could scarcely stand. However, he was very courageous and after he had been walking about three hours, he arrived at the Doctor's house, and knocked at the door.

"'Who is there?' cried the Doctor, putting his head out of his bedroom window.

"'Little Hans, Doctor.'

"'What do you want, little Hans?'

"'The Miller's son has fallen from a ladder, and has hurt himself, and the Miller wants you to come at once.'

"'All right!' said the Doctor; and he ordered his horse, and his big boots, and his lantern, and came downstairs, and rode off in the direction of the Miller's house, little Hans trudging behind him.

"But the storm grew worse and worse, and the rain fell in torrents, and little Hans could not see where he was going, or keep up with the horse. At last he lost his way, and wandered off on the moor, which was a very dangerous place, as it was full of deep holes, and there poor little Hans was drowned. His body was found the next day by some goatherds, floating in a great pool of water, and was brought back by them to the cottage.

"Everybody went to little Hans's funeral, as he was so popular, and the Miller was the chief mourner.

"'As I was his best friend,' said the Miller, 'it is only fair that I should have the best place;' so he walked at the head of the procession in a long black cloak, and every now and then he wiped his eyes with a big pocket-handkerchief.

"'Little Hans is certainly a great loss to every one,' said the Blacksmith, when the funeral was over, and they were all seated comfortably in the inn, drinking spiced wine and eating sweet cakes.

'A great loss to me at any rate,' answered the Miller; 'why, I had as good as given him my wheelbarrow, and now I really don't know what to do with it. It is very much in my way at home, and it is in such bad repair that I could not get anything for it if I sold it. I will certainly take care not to give away anything again. One always suffers for being generous.'"

"Well?" said the Water-rat, after a long pause.

"Well, that is the end," said the Linnet.

"But what became of the Miller?" asked the Water-rat.

"Oh! I really don't know," replied the Linnet; "and I am sure that I don't care."

"It is quite evident then that you have no sympathy in your nature," said the Water-rat.

"I am afraid you don't quite see the moral of the story," remarked the Linnet.

"The what?" screamed the Water-rat.

"The moral."

"Do you mean to say that the story has a moral?"

"Certainly," said the Linnet.

"Well, really," said the Water-rat, in a very angry manner, "I think you should have told me that before you began. If you had done so, I certainly would not have listened to you; in fact, I should have said 'Pooh', like the critic. However, I can say it now;" so he shouted out "Pooh" at the top of his voice, gave a whisk with his tail, and went back into his hole.

"And how do you like the Water-rat?" asked the Duck, who came paddling up some minutes afterwards. "He has a great many good points, but for my own part I have a mother's feelings, and I can never look at a confirmed bachelor without the tears coming into my eyes."

"I am rather afraid that I have annoyed him," answered the Linnet. "The fact is, that I told him a story with a moral."

"Ah! that is always a very dangerous thing to do," said the Duck. And I quite agree with her.

THE SELFISH GIANT

EVERY AFTERNOON, as they were coming from school, the children used to go and play in the Giant's garden.

It was a large lovely garden, with soft green grass. Here and there over the grass stood beautiful flowers like stars, and there were twelve peach-trees that in the spring-time broke out into delicate blossoms of pink and pearl, and in the autumn bore rich fruit. The birds sat on the trees and sang so sweetly that the children used to stop their games in order to listen to them. "How happy we are here!" they cried to each other.

One day the Giant came back. He had been to visit his friend the Cornish ogre, and had stayed with him for seven years. After the seven years were over he had said all that he had to say, for his conversation was limited, and he determined to return to his own castle. When he arrived he saw the children playing in the garden.

"What are you doing there?" he cried in a very gruff voice, and the children ran away.

"My own garden is my own garden," said the Giant; "any one can understand that, and I will allow nobody to play in it but myself." So he built a high wall all round it, and put up a notice-board.

> **TRESPASSERS WILL BE PROSECUTED**

He was a very selfish Giant. The poor children had now nowhere to play. They tried to play on the road, but the road was very dusty and full of hard stones, and they did not like it. They used to wander round the high wall when their lessons were over, and talk about the beautiful garden inside. "How happy we were there," they said to each other.

Then the Spring came, and all over the country there were little blossoms and little birds. Only in the garden of the Selfish Giant it was still winter. The birds did not care to sing in it as there were no children, and the trees forgot to blossom. Once a beautiful flower put its head out from the grass, but when it saw the notice-board it was so sorry for the children that it slipped back into the ground again, and went off to sleep. The only people who were pleased were the Snow and the Frost. "Spring has forgotten this garden," they cried, "so we will live here all the year round." The Snow covered up the grass with her great white cloak, and the Frost painted all the trees silver. Then they invited the North Wind to stay with them, and he came. He was wrapped in furs, and he roared all day about the garden, and blew the chimney-pots down. "This is a delightful spot," he said, "we must ask the Hail on a visit." So the Hail came. Every day for three hours he rattled on the roof of the castle till he broke most of the slates, and then he ran round and round the garden as fast as he could go. He was dressed in grey, and his breath was like ice.

"I cannot understand why the Spring is so late in coming," said the Selfish Giant, as he sat at the window and looked out at his cold white garden; "I hope there will be a change in the weather."

But the Spring never came, nor the Summer. The Autumn gave golden fruit to every garden, but to the Giant's garden she gave none. "He is too selfish," she said. So it was always Winter there, and the North Wind and the Hail, and the Frost, and the Snow danced about through the trees.

One morning the Giant was lying awake in bed when he heard some lovely music. It sounded so sweet to his ears that he thought it must be the King's musicians passing by. It was really only a little linnet singing outside his window, but it was so long since he had heard a bird sing in his garden that it seemed to him to be the most beautiful music in the world. Then the Hail stopped dancing over his head, and the North Wind ceased roaring, and a delicious perfume came to him through the open casement. "I believe the Spring has come at last," said the Giant; and he jumped out of bed and looked out.

What did he see?

He saw a most wonderful sight. Through a little hole in the wall the children had crept in, and they were sitting in the branches of the trees. In every tree that he could see there was a little child. And the trees were so glad to have the children back again that they had covered themselves with blossoms, and were waving their arms gently above the children's heads. The birds were flying about and twittering with delight, and the flowers were looking up through the green grass and laughing. It was a lovely scene, only in one corner it was still winter. It was the farthest corner of the garden, and in it was standing a little boy. He was so small that he could not reach up to the branches of the tree, and he was

wandering all round it, crying bitterly. The poor tree was still quite covered with frost and snow, and the North Wind was blowing and roaring above it. "Climb up! little boy," said the Tree, and it bent its branches down as low as it could; but the boy was too tiny.

And the Giant's heart melted as he looked out. "How selfish I have been!" he said; "now I know why the Spring would not come here. I will put that poor little boy on the top of the tree, and then I will knock down the wall, and my garden shall be the children's playground for ever and ever." He was really very sorry for what he had done.

So he crept downstairs and opened the front door quite softly, and went out into the garden. But when the children saw him they were so frightened that they all ran away, and the garden became winter again. Only the little boy did not run, for his eyes

were so full of tears that he did not see the Giant coming. And the Giant stole up behind him and took him gently in his hand, and put him up into the tree. And the tree broke at once into blossom, and the birds came and sang on it, and the little boy stretched out his two arms and flung them round the Giant's neck, and kissed him. And the other children, when they saw that the Giant was not wicked any longer, came running back, and with them came the Spring. "It is your garden now, little children," said the Giant, and he took a great axe and knocked down the wall. And when the people were going to market at twelve o'clock they found the Giant playing with the children in the most beautiful garden they had ever seen.

All day long they played, and in the evening they came to the Giant to bid him good-bye.

"But where is your little companion?" he said: "the boy I put into the tree." The Giant loved him the best because he had kissed him.

"We don't know," answered the children; "he has gone away."

"You must tell him to be sure and come here to-morrow," said the Giant. But the children said that they did not know where he lived, and had never seen him before; and the Giant felt very sad.

Every afternoon, when school was over, the children came and played with the Giant. But the little boy whom the Giant loved was never seen again. The Giant was very kind to all the children, yet he longed for his first little friend, and often spoke of him. "How I would like to see him!" he used to say.

Years went over, and the Giant grew very old and feeble. He could not play about any more, so he sat in a huge armchair, and watched the children at their games, and admired his garden. "I have many beautiful flowers," he said; "but the children are the most beautiful flowers of all."

One winter morning he looked out of his window as he was dressing. He did not hate the Winter now, for he knew that it was merely the Spring asleep, and that the flowers were resting.

Suddenly he rubbed his eyes in wonder, and looked and looked. It certainly was a marvellous sight. In the farthest corner of the garden was a tree quite covered with lovely white blossoms. Its branches were all golden, and silver fruit hung down from them, and underneath it stood the little boy he had loved.

Downstairs ran the Giant in great joy, and out into the garden. He hastened across the grass, and came near to the child. And when he came quite close his face grew red with anger, and he said, "Who hath dared to wound thee?" For on the palms of the child's hands were the prints of two nails, and the prints of two nails were on the little feet.

"Who hath dared to wound thee?" cried the Giant; "tell me, that I may take my big sword and slay him."

"Nay!" answered the child; "but these are the wounds of Love."

"Who art thou?" said the Giant, and a strange awe fell on him, and he knelt before the little child.

And the child smiled on the Giant, and said to him, "You let me play once in your garden, to-day you shall come with me to my garden, which is Paradise."

And when the children ran in that afternoon, they found the Giant lying dead under the tree, all covered with white blossoms.

THE REMARKABLE ROCKET

THE KING'S SON was going to be married, so there were general rejoicings. He had waited a whole year for his bride, and at last she had arrived. She was a Russian Princess, and had driven all the way from Finland in a sledge drawn by six reindeer. The sledge was shaped like a great golden swan, and between the swan's wings lay the little Princess herself. Her long ermine cloak reached right down to her feet, on her head was a tiny cap of silver tissue, and she was as pale as the Snow Palace in which she had always lived. So pale was she that as she drove through the streets all the people wondered. "She is like a white rose!" they cried, and they threw down flowers on her from the balconies.

At the gate of the Castle the Prince was waiting to receive her. He had dreamy violet eyes and his hair was like fine gold. When he saw her he sank upon one knee, and kissed her hand.

"Your picture was beautiful," he murmured, "but you are more beautiful than your picture;" and the little Princess blushed.

"She was like a white rose before," said a young Page to his neighbour, "but she is like a red rose now;" and the whole Court was delighted.

For the next three days everybody went about saying, "White rose, Red rose, Red rose, White rose;" and the King gave orders that the Page's salary was to be doubled. As he received no salary at all this was not of much use to him, but it was considered a great honour, and was duly published in the Court Gazette.

When the three days were over the marriage was celebrated. It was a magnificent ceremony, and the bride and bridegroom walked hand in hand under a canopy of purple embroidered with little pearls. Then there was a State Banquet, which lasted for five hours. The Prince and Princess sat at the top of the Great Hall and drank out of a cup of clear crystal. Only true lovers could drink out of this cup, for if false lips touched it, it grew grey and dull and cloudy.

"It is quite clear that they love each other," said the little Page, "as clear as crystal!" and the King doubled his salary a second time. "What an honour!" cried all the courtiers.

After the banquet there was to be a Ball. The bride and bridegroom were to dance the Rose-dance together, and the King had promised to play the flute. He played very badly, but no one had ever dared to tell him so, because he was the King. Indeed, he only knew two airs, and was never quite certain which one he was playing; but it made no matter, for, whatever he did, everybody cried out, "Charming! charming!"

The last item on the programme was a grand display of fireworks, to be let off exactly at midnight. The little Princess had never seen a firework in her life, so the King had given orders that the Royal Pyrotechnist should be in attendance on the day of her marriage.

"What are fireworks like?" she had asked the Prince, one morning, as she was walking on the terrace.

"They are like the Aurora Borealis," said the King, who always answered questions that were addressed to other people, "only much more natural. I prefer them to stars myself, as you always know when they are going to appear, and they are as delightful as my own flute-playing. You must certainly see them."

So at the end of the King's garden a great stand had been set up, and as soon as the Royal Pyrotechnist had put everything in its proper place, the fireworks began to talk to each other.

"The world is certainly very beautiful," cried a little Squib. "Just look at those yellow tulips. Why! if they were real crackers they could not be lovelier. I am very glad I have travelled. Travel improves the mind wonderfully, and does away with all one's prejudices."

"The King's garden is not the world, you foolish squib," said a big Roman Candle; "the world is an enormous place, and it would take you three days to see it thoroughly."

"Any place you love is the world to you," exclaimed a pensive Catherine Wheel, who had been attached to an old deal box in early life, and prided herself on her broken heart; "but love is not fashionable any more, the poets have killed it. They wrote so much about it that nobody believed them, and I am not surprised. True love suffers, and is silent. I remember myself once – but it is no matter now. Romance is a thing of the past."

"Nonsense!" said the Roman Candle. "Romance never dies. It is like the moon, and lives for ever. The bride and bridegroom, for instance, love each other very dearly. I heard all about them this morning from a brown-paper cartridge, who happened to be staying in the same drawer as myself, and knew the latest Court news."

But the Catherine Wheel shook her head. "Romance is dead, Romance is dead," she murmured. She was one of those people who think that, if you say the same thing over and over a great many times, it becomes true in the end.

Suddenly, a sharp, dry cough was heard, and they all looked round.

It came from a tall, supercilious-looking Rocket, who was tied to the end of a long stick. He always coughed before he made any observation, so as to attract attention.

"Ahem! ahem!" he said, and everybody listened except the poor Catherine Wheel, who was still shaking her head, and murmuring, "Romance is dead."

"Order! order!" cried out a Cracker. He was something of a politician, and had always taken a prominent part in the local elections, so he knew the proper Parliamentary expressions to use.

"Quite dead," whispered the Catherine Wheel, and she went off to sleep.

As soon as there was perfect silence, the Rocket coughed a third time and began. He spoke with a very slow, distinct voice, as if he were dictating his memoirs, and always looked over the shoulder of the person to whom he was talking. In fact, he had a most distinguished manner.

"How fortunate it is for the King's son," he remarked, "that he is to be married on the very day on which I am to be let off. Really, if it had been arranged beforehand, it could not have turned out better for him; but Princes are always lucky."

"Dear me!" said the little Squib, "I thought it was quite the other way, and that we were to be let off in the Prince's honour."

"It may be so with you," he answered; "indeed, I have no doubt that it is, but with me it is different. I am a very remarkable Rocket, and come of remarkable parents. My mother was the most celebrated Catherine Wheel of her day, and was renowned for her graceful dancing. When she made her great public appearance she spun round nineteen times before she went out, and each time that she did so she threw into the air seven pink stars. She was three feet and a half in diameter, and made of the very best gunpowder. My father was a Rocket like myself, and of French extraction. He flew so high that the people were afraid that he would never come down again. He did, though, for he was of a kindly disposition, and he made a most brilliant descent in a shower of golden rain. The newspapers wrote about his performance in very flattering terms. Indeed, the Court Gazette called him a triumph of Pylotechnic art."

"Pyrotechnic, Pyrotechnic, you mean," said a Bengal Light; "I know it is Pyrotechnic, for I saw it written on my own canister."

"Well, I said Pylotechnic," answered the Rocket, in a severe tone of voice, and the Bengal Light felt so crushed that he began at once to bully the little Squibs, in order to show that he was still a person of some importance.

"I was saying," continued the Rocket, "I was saying – what was I saying?"

"You were talking about yourself," replied the Roman Candle.

"Of course; I knew I was discussing some interesting subject when I was so rudely interrupted. I hate rudeness and bad manners of every kind, for I am extremely sensitive. No one in the whole world is so sensitive as I am, I am quite sure of that."

"What is a sensitive person?" said the Cracker to the Roman Candle.

"A person who, because he has corns himself, always treads on other people's toes," answered the Roman Candle in a low whisper; and the Cracker nearly exploded with laughter.

"Pray, what are you laughing at?" inquired the Rocket; "I am not laughing."

"I am laughing because I am happy," replied the Cracker.

"That is a very selfish reason," said the Rocket angrily. "What right have you to be happy? You should be thinking about others. In fact, you should be thinking about me. I am always thinking about myself, and I expect everybody else to do the same. That is what is called sympathy. It is a beautiful virtue, and I possess it in a high degree. Suppose, for instance, anything happened to me to-night, what a misfortune that would be for every one! The Prince and Princess

 would never be happy again, their whole married life would be spoiled; and as for the King, I know he would not get over it. Really, when I begin to reflect on the importance of my position, I am almost moved to tears."

"If you want to give pleasure to others," cried the Roman Candle, "you had better keep yourself dry."

"Certainly," exclaimed the Bengal Light, who was now in better spirits; "that is only common sense."

"Common sense, indeed!" said the Rocket indignantly; "you forget that I am very uncommon, and very remarkable. Why, anybody can have common sense, provided that they have no imagination. But I have imagination, for I never think of things as they really are; I always think of them as being quite different. As for keeping myself dry, there is evidently no one here who can at all appreciate an emotional nature. Fortunately for myself, I don't care. The only thing that sustains one through life is the consciousness of the immense inferiority of everybody else, and this is a feeling that I have always cultivated. But none of you have any hearts. Here you are laughing and making merry just as if the Prince and Princess had not just been married."

"Well, really," exclaimed a small Fire-balloon, "why not? It is a most joyful occasion, and when I soar up into the air I intend to tell the stars all about it. You will see them twinkle when I talk to them about the pretty bride."

"Ah! what a trivial view of life!" said the Rocket; "but it is only what I expected. There is nothing in you; you are hollow and empty. Why, perhaps the Prince and Princess may go to live in a country where there is a deep river, and perhaps they may have one only son, a little fair-haired boy with violet eyes like the Prince himself; and perhaps some day he may go out to walk with his nurse; and perhaps the nurse may go to sleep under a great elder-tree; and perhaps the little boy may fall into the deep river and be drowned. What a terrible misfortune! Poor people, to lose their only son! It is really too dreadful! I shall never get over it."

"But they have not lost their only son," said the Roman Candle; "no misfortune has happened to them at all."

"I never said that they had," replied the Rocket; "I said that they might. If they had lost their only son there would be no use in saying anything more about the matter. I hate people who cry over spilt milk. But when I think that they might lose their only son, I certainly am very much affected."

"You certainly are!" cried the Bengal Light. "In fact, you are the most affected person I ever met."

"You are the rudest person I ever met," said the Rocket, "and you cannot understand my friendship for the Prince."

"Why, you don't even know him," growled the Roman Candle.

"I never said I knew him," answered the Rocket. "I dare say that if I knew him I should not be his friend at all. It is a very dangerous thing to know one's friends."

"You had really better keep yourself dry," said the Fireballoon. "That is the important thing."

"Very important for you, I have no doubt," answered the Rocket, "but I shall weep if I choose;" and he actually burst into real tears, which flowed down his stick like raindrops, and nearly drowned two little beetles, who were just thinking of setting up house together, and were looking for a nice dry spot to live in.

"He must have a truly romantic nature," said the Catherine Wheel, "for he weeps when there is nothing at all to weep about;" and she heaved a deep sigh, and thought about the deal box.

But the Roman Candle and the Bengal Light were quite indignant, and kept saying, "Humbug! humbug!" at the top of their voices. They were extremely practical, and whenever they objected to anything they called it humbug.

Then the moon rose like a wonderful silver shield; and the stars began to shine, and a sound of music came from the palace.

The Prince and Princess were leading the dance. They danced so beautifully that the tall white lilies peeped in at the window and watched them, and the great red poppies nodded their heads and beat time.

Then ten o'clock struck, and then eleven, and then twelve, and at the last stroke of midnight every one came out on the terrace, and the King sent for the Royal Pyrotechnist.

"Let the fireworks begin," said the King; and the Royal Pyrotechnist made a low bow, and marched down to the end of the garden. He had six attendants with him, each of whom carried a lighted torch at the end of a long pole.

It was certainly a magnificent display.

Whizz! Whizz! went the Catherine Wheel, as she spun round

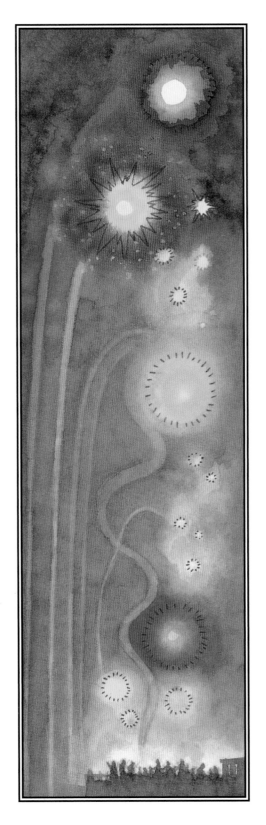

and round. Boom! Boom! went the Roman Candle. Then the Squibs danced all over the place, and the Bengal Lights made everything look scarlet. "Goodbye," cried the Fire-balloon, as he soared away dropping tiny blue sparks. Bang! Bang! answered the Crackers, who were enjoying themselves immensely. Every one was a great success except the Remarkable Rocket. He was so damp with crying that he could not go off at all. The best thing in him was the gunpowder, and that was so wet with tears that it was of no use. All his poor relations, to whom he would never speak, except with a sneer, shot up into the sky like wonderful golden flowers with blossoms of fire. Huzza! Huzza! cried the Court; and the little Princess laughed with pleasure.

"I suppose they are reserving me for some grand occasion," said the Rocket; "no doubt that is what it means," and he looked more supercilious than ever.

The next day the workmen came to put everything tidy.

"This is evidently a deputation," said the Rocket; "I will receive them with becoming dignity": so he put his nose in the air, and began to frown severely as if he were thinking about some very important subject. But they took no notice of him at all till they were just going away. Then one of them caught sight of him. "Hello!" he cried, "what a bad rocket!" and he threw him over the wall into the ditch.

"BAD Rocket?" he said as he whirled through the air; "impossible! GRAND Rocket, that is what the man said. BAD and GRAND sound very much the same, indeed they often are the same;" and he fell into the mud.

"It is not comfortable here," he remarked, "but no doubt it is some fashionable watering place, and they have sent me away to restore my health. My nerves are certainly very much shattered, and I require rest."

Then a little Frog, with bright jewelled eyes, and a green mottled coat, swam up to him.

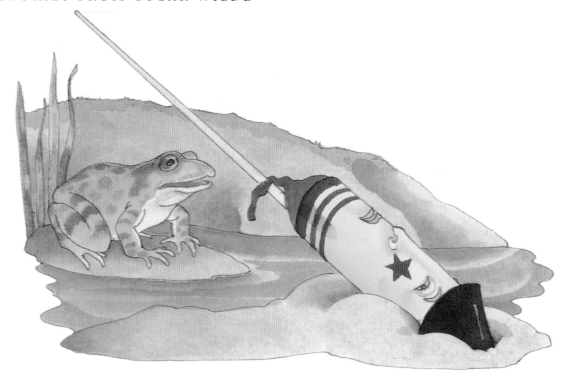

"A new arrival, I see!" said the Frog. "Well, after all there is nothing like mud. Give me rainy weather and a ditch, and I am quite happy. Do you think it will be a wet afternoon? I am sure I hope so, but the sky is quite blue and cloudless. What a pity!"

"Ahem! ahem!" said the Rocket, and he began to cough.

"What a delightful voice you have!" cried the Frog. "Really it is quite like a croak, and croaking is of course the most musical sound in the world. You will hear our glee-club this evening. We sit in the old duck-pond close by the farmer's house, and as soon as the moon rises we begin. It is so entrancing that everybody lies awake to listen to us. In fact, it was only yesterday that I heard the farmer's wife say to her mother that she could not get a wink of sleep at night on account of us. It is most gratifying to find oneself so popular."

"Ahem! ahem!" said the Rocket angrily. He was very much annoyed that he could not get a word in.

"A delightful voice, certainly," continued the Frog; "I hope you will come over to the duck-pond. I am off to look for my daughters. I have six beautiful daughters, and I am so afraid the

Pike may meet them. He is a perfect monster, and would have no hesitation in breakfasting off them. Well, good-bye: I have enjoyed our conversation very much, I assure you."

"Conversation, indeed!" said the Rocket. "You have talked the whole time yourself. That is not conversation."

"Somebody must listen," answered the Frog, "and I like to do all the talking myself. It saves time, and prevents arguments."

"But I like arguments," said the Rocket.

"I hope not," said the Frog complacently. "Arguments are extremely vulgar, for everybody in good society holds exactly the same opinions. Good-bye a second time; I see my daughters in the distance;" and the little Frog swam away.

"You are a very irritating person," said the Rocket, "and very ill-bred. I hate people who talk about themselves, as you do, when one wants to talk about oneself, as I do. It is what I call selfishness, and selfishness is a most detestable thing, especially to any one of my temperament, for I am well known for my sympathetic nature. In fact, you should take example by me, you could not possibly have a better model. Now that you have the chance you had better avail yourself of it, for I am going back to Court almost immediately. I am a great favourite at Court; in fact, the Prince and Princess were married yesterday in my honour. Of course you know nothing of these matters, for you are a provincial."

"There is no good talking to him," said a Dragon-fly, who was sitting on the top of a large brown bulrush; "no good at all, for he has gone away."

"Well, that is his loss, not mine," answered the Rocket. "I am not going to stop talking to him merely because he pays no attention. I like hearing myself talk. It is one of my greatest pleasures. I often have long conversations all by myself, and I am so clever that sometimes I don't understand a single word of what I am saying."

"Then you should certainly lecture on Philosophy," said the Dragon-fly; and he spread a pair of lovely gauze wings and soared away into the sky.

"How very silly of him not to stay here!" said the Rocket. "I am sure that he has not often got such a chance of improving his mind. However, I don't care a bit. Genius like mine is sure to be appreciated some day;" and he sank down a little deeper into the mud.

After some time a large White Duck swam up to him. She had yellow legs, and webbed feet, and was considered a great beauty on account of her waddle.

"Quack, quack, quack," she said. "What a curious shape you are! May I ask were you born like that, or is it the result of an accident?"

"It is quite evident that you have always lived in the country," answered the Rocket, "otherwise you would know who I am. However, I excuse your ignorance. It would be unfair to expect other people to be as remarkable as oneself. You will no doubt be surprised to hear that I can fly up into the sky, and come down in a shower of golden rain."

"I don't think much of that," said the Duck, "as I cannot see what use it is to any one. Now, if you could plough the fields like the ox, or draw a cart like the horse, or look after the sheep like the collie-dog that would be something."

"My good creature," cried the Rocket in a very haughty tone of voice, "I see that you belong to the lower orders. A person of my position is never useful. We have certain accomplishments, and that is more than sufficient. I have no sympathy myself with industry of any kind, least of all with such industries as you seem to recommend. Indeed, I have always been of the opinion that hard work is simply the refuge of people who have nothing whatever to do."

"Well, well," said the Duck, who was of a very peaceable disposition, and never quarrelled with any one, "everybody has different tastes. I hope, at any rate, that you are going to take up your residence here."

"Oh! dear no," cried the Rocket. "I am merely a visitor, a distinguished visitor. The fact is that I find this place rather tedious. There is neither society here, nor solitude. In fact, it is essentially suburban. I shall probably go back to Court, for I know that I am destined to make a sensation in the world."

"I had thoughts of entering public life once myself," remarked the Duck; "there are so many things that need reforming. Indeed, I took the chair at a meeting some time ago, and we passed resolutions condemning everything that we did not like. However, they did not seem to have much effect. Now I go in for domesticity, and look after my family."

"I am made for public life," said the Rocket, "and so are all my relations, even the humblest of them. Whenever we appear we excite great attention. I have not actually appeared myself, but when I do so it will be a magnificent sight. As for domesticity, it ages one rapidly, and distracts one's mind from higher things."

"Ah! the higher things of life, how fine they are!" said the Duck; "and that reminds me how hungry I feel," and she swam away down the stream, saying, "Quack, quack, quack."

"Come back! come back!" screamed the Rocket, "I have a great deal to say to you;" but the Duck paid no attention to him. "I am glad that she has gone," he said to himself, "she has a decidedly middle-class mind;" and he sank a little deeper still into the mud, and began to think about the loneliness of genius, when suddenly two little boys in white smocks came running down the bank, with a kettle and some faggots.

"This must be the deputation," said the Rocket, and he tried to look very dignified.

"Hallo!" cried one of the boys, "look at this old stick! I wonder how it came here;" and he picked the rocket out of the ditch.

"OLD Stick!" said the Rocket, "impossible! GOLD Stick, that is what he said. Gold Stick is very complimentary. In fact, he mistakes me for one of the Court dignitaries!"

"Let us put it into the fire!" said the other boy, "it will help to boil the kettle."

So they piled the faggots together, and put the Rocket on top, and lit the fire.

"This is magnificent," cried the Rocket, "they are going to let me off in broad daylight, so that every one can see me."

"We will go to sleep now," they said, "and when we wake up the kettle will be boiled;" and they lay down on the grass, and shut their eyes.

The Rocket was very damp, so he took a long time to burn. At last, however, the fire caught him.

"Now I am going off!" he cried, and he made himself very stiff and straight. "I know I shall go much higher than the stars, much higher than the moon, much higher than the sun. In fact, I shall go so high that—"

Fizz! Fizz! Fizz! and he went straight up into the air.

"Delightful!" he cried, "I shall go on like this for ever. What a success I am!"

But nobody saw him.

Then he began to feel a curious tingling sensation all over him.

"Now I am going to explode," he cried. "I shall set the whole world on fire, and make such a noise, that nobody will talk about anything else for a whole year." And he certainly did explode. Bang! Bang! Bang! went the gunpowder. There was no doubt about it.

But nobody heard him, not even the two little boys, for they were sound asleep.

Then all that was left of him was the stick, and this fell down on the back of a Goose who was taking walk by the side of the ditch.

"Good heavens!" cried the Goose. "It is going to rain sticks;" and she rushed into the water.

"I knew I should create a great sensation," gasped the Rocket, and he went out.

THE YOUNG KING

IT WAS THE NIGHT before the day fixed for his coronation, and the young King was sitting alone in his beautiful chamber. His courtiers had all taken their leave of him, bowing their heads to the ground, according to the ceremonious usage of the day, and had retired to the Great Hall of the Palace, to receive a few last lessons from the Professor of Etiquette; there being some of them who had still quite natural manners, which in a courtier is, I need hardly say, a very grave offence.

The lad – for he was only a lad, being but sixteen years of age – was not sorry at their departure, and had flung himself back with a deep sigh of relief on the soft cushions of his embroidered couch, lying there, wild-eyed and open-mouthed, like a brown woodland Faun, or some young animal of the forest newly snared by the hunters.

And, indeed, it was the hunters who had found him, coming upon him almost by chance as, bare-limbed and pipe in hand, he

was following the flock of the poor goatherd who had brought him up, and whose son he had always fancied himself to be. The child of the old King's only daughter by a secret marriage with one much beneath her in station – a stranger, some said, who, by the wonderful magic of his lute-playing, had made the young Princess love him; while others spoke of an artist from Rimini, to whom the Princess had shown much, perhaps too much honour, and who had suddenly disappeared from the city, leaving his work in the Cathedral unfinished – he had been, when but a week old, stolen away from his mother's side, as she slept, and given into the charge of a common peasant and his wife, who were without children of their own, and lived in a remote part of the forest, more than a day's ride from the town. Grief, or the plague, as the court physician stated, or, as some suggested, a swift Italian poison administered in a cup of spiced wine, slew, within an hour of her wakening, the white girl who had given him birth, and as the trusty messenger who bore the child across his saddle-bow, stooped from his weary horse and knocked at the rude door of the goatherd's hut, the body of the Princess was being lowered into an open grave that had been dug in a deserted churchyard, beyond the city gates, a grave where, it was said, another body was also lying, that of a young man of marvellous and foreign beauty, whose hands were tied behind him with a knotted cord, and whose breast was stabbed with many red wounds.

Such, at least, was the story that men whispered to each other. Certain it was that the old King, when on his death-bed, whether moved by remorse for his great sin, or merely desiring that the kingdom should not pass away from his line, had had the lad sent for, and, in the presence of the Council, had acknowledged him as his heir.

And it seems that from the very first moment of his recognition he had shown signs of that strange passion for beauty that was destined to have so great an influence over his life. Those who accompanied him to the suite of rooms set apart for his service, often spoke of the cry of pleasure that broke from his lips when he saw the delicate raiment and rich jewels that had been prepared for him, and of the almost fierce joy with which he flung aside his rough leathern tunic and coarse sheepskin cloak. He missed, indeed, at times the fine freedom of his forest life, and was always apt to chafe at the tedious Court ceremonies that occupied so much of each day, but the wonderful place – Joyeuse, as they called it – of which he now found himself lord, seemed to him to be a new world fresh-fashioned for his delight; and as soon as he could escape from the council-board or audience-chamber, he would run down the great staircase, with its lions of gilt bronze and its steps of bright porphyry, and wander from room to room, and from corridor to corridor, like one who was seeking to find in beauty an anodyne from pain, a sort of restoration from sickness.

Upon these journeys of discovery, as he would call them – and, indeed, they were to him real voyages through a marvellous land, he would sometimes be accompanied by the slim, fair-haired Court pages, with their floating mantles, and gay fluttering ribands; but more often he would be alone, feeling through a certain quick instinct, which was almost a divination, that the secrets of art are best learned in secret, and that Beauty, like Wisdom, loves the lonely worshipper.

Many curious stories were related about him at this period. It was said that a stout Burgomaster, who had come to deliver a florid oratorical address on behalf of the citizens of the town, had caught sight of him kneeling in real adoration before a great picture that had just been brought from Venice, and that seemed to herald the worship of some new gods. On another occasion he had been missed for several hours, and after a lengthened search had been discovered in a little chamber in one of the northern turrets of the palace gazing, as one in a trance, at a Greek gem carved with the figure of Adonis. He had been seen, so the tale ran, pressing his warm lips to the marble brow of an antique statue that had been discovered in the bed of the river on the occasion of the building of the stone bridge, and was inscribed with the name of the Bithynian slave of Hadrian. He had passed a whole night in noting the effect of the moonlight on a silver image of Endymion.

All rare and costly materials had certainly a great fascination for him, and in his eagerness to procure them he had sent away many merchants, some to traffic for amber with the rough fisher-folk of the north seas, some to Egypt to look for that curious green turquoise which is found only in the tombs of kings, and is said to possess magical properties, some to Persia for silken carpets and painted pottery, and others to India to buy gauze and stained ivory, moonstones and bracelets of jade, sandalwood and blue enamel and shawls of fine wool.

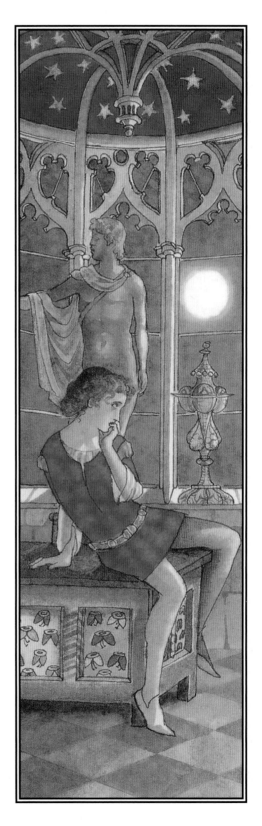

But what had occupied him most was the robe he was to wear at his coronation, the robe of tissued gold, and the ruby-studded crown, and the sceptre with its rows and rings of pearls. Indeed, it was of this that he was thinking to-night, as he lay back on his luxurious couch, watching the great pinewood log that was burning itself out on the open hearth. The designs, which were from the hands of the most famous artists of the time, had been submitted to him many months before, and he had given orders that the artificers were to toil night and day to carry them out, and that the whole world was to be searched for jewels that would be worthy of their work. He saw himself in fancy standing at the high altar of the cathedral in the fair raiment of a King, and a smile played and lingered about his boyish lips, and lit up with a bright lustre his dark woodland eyes.

After some time he rose from his seat, and leaning against the carved penthouse of the chimney, looked round at the dimly-lit room. The walls were hung with rich tapestries representing the Triumph of Beauty. A large press, inlaid with agate and lapis-lazuli, filled one corner, and facing the window stood a curiously

wrought cabinet with lacquer panels of powdered and mosaicked gold, on which were placed some delicate goblets of Venetian glass, and a cup of dark-veined onyx. Pale poppies were broidered on the silk coverlet of the bed, as though they had fallen from the tired hands of sleep, and tall reeds of fluted ivory bore up the velvet canopy, from which great tufts of ostrich plumes sprang, like white foam, to the pallid silver of the fretted ceiling. A laughing Narcissus in green bronze held a polished mirror above its head. On the table stood a flat bowl of amethyst.

Outside he could see the huge dome of the cathedral, looming like a bubble over the shadowy houses, and the weary sentinels pacing up and down on the misty terrace by the river. Far away, in an orchard, a nightingale was singing. A faint perfume of jasmine came through the open window. He brushed his brown curls back from his forehead, and taking up a lute, let his fingers stray across the cords. His heavy eyelids drooped, and a strange languor came over him. Never before had he felt so keenly, or with such exquisite joy, the magic and the mystery of beautiful things.

When midnight sounded from the clock-tower he touched a bell, and his pages entered and disrobed him with much ceremony, pouring rose-water over his hands, and strewing flowers on his pillow. A few moments after they had left the room, he fell asleep.

And as he slept he dreamed a dream, and this was his dream.

He thought that he was standing in a long, low attic, amidst the whirr and clatter of many looms. The meagre daylight peered in through the grated windows, and showed him the gaunt figures of the weavers bending over their cases. Pale, sickly-looking children were crouched on the huge cross-beams. As the shuttles dashed through the warp they lifted up

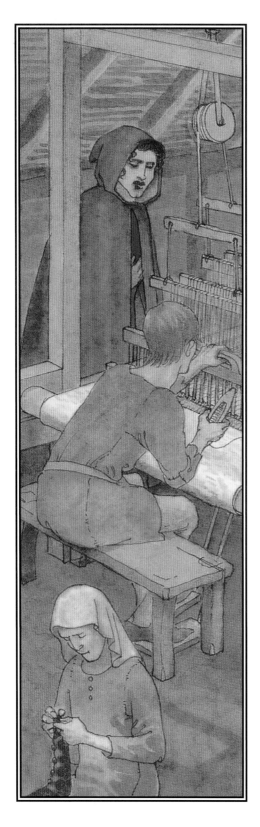

the heavy battens, and when the shuttles stopped they let the battens fall and pressed the threads together. Their faces were pinched with famine, and their thin hands shook and trembled. Some haggard women were seated at a table sewing. A horrible odour filled the place. The air was foul and heavy, and the walls dripped and streamed with damp.

The young King went over to one of the weavers, and stood by him and watched him.

And the weaver looked at him angrily, and said, "Why art thou watching me? Art thou a spy set on us by our master?"

"Who is thy master?" asked the young King.

"Our master!" cried the weaver, bitterly. "He is a man like myself. Indeed, there is but this difference between us – that he wears fine clothes while I go in rags, and that while I am weak from hunger he suffers not a little from overfeeding."

"The land is free," said the young King, "and thou art no man's slave."

 "In war," answered the weaver, "the strong make slaves of the weak, and in peace the rich make slaves of the poor. We must work to live, and they give us such mean wages that we die. We toil for them all day long, and they heap up gold in their coffers, and our children fade away before their time, and the faces of those we love become hard and evil. We tread out the grapes, and another drinks the wine. We sow the corn, and our own board is empty. We have chains, though no eye beholds them; and are slaves, though men call us free."

"Is it so with all?" he asked.

"It is so with all," answered the weaver, "with the young as well as with the old, with the women as well as with the men, with the little children as well as with those who are stricken in years. The merchants grind us down, and we must needs do their bidding. The priest rides by and tells his beads, and no man has care of us. Through our sunless lanes creeps Poverty with her hungry eyes, and Sin with his sodden face follows close behind her. Misery wakes us in the morning, and Shame sits with us at night. But what are these things to thee? Thou art not one of us. Thy face is too happy." And he turned away scowling, and threw the shuttle across the loom, and the young King saw that it was threaded with a thread of gold.

And a great terror seized upon him, and he said to the weaver, "What robe is this that thou art weaving?"

"It is the robe for the coronation of the young King," he answered; "what is that to thee?"

And the young King gave a loud cry and woke, and lo! he was in his own chamber, and through the window he saw the great honey-coloured moon hanging in the dusky air.

And he fell asleep again and dreamed, and this was his dream.

He thought that he was lying on the deck of a huge galley that was being rowed by a hundred slaves. On a carpet by his side the master of the galley was seated. He was black as ebony, and his turban was of crimson silk. Great earrings of silver dragged down the thick lobes of his ears, and in his hands he had a pair of ivory scales.

The slaves were naked, but for a ragged loincloth, and each man was chained to his neighbour. The hot sun beat brightly upon them, and the Negroes ran up and down the gangway and lashed them with whips of hide. They stretched out their lean arms and pulled the heavy oars through the water. The salt spray flew from the blades.

At last they reached a little bay, and began to take soundings. A light wind blew from the shore, and covered the deck and the great lateen sail with a fine red dust. Three Arabs mounted on wild asses rode out and threw spears at them. The master of the galley took a painted bow in his hand and shot one of them in the throat. He fell heavily into the surf, and his companions galloped away.

A woman wrapped in a yellow veil followed slowly on a camel, looking back now and then at the dead body.

As soon as they had cast anchor and hauled down sail, the Negroes went into the hold and brought up a long rope-ladder, heavily weighted with lead. The master of the galley threw it over the side, making the ends fast to two iron stanchions. Then the Negroes seized the youngest of the slaves, and knocked his gyves off, and filled his nostrils and his ears with wax, and tied a big stone round his waist. He crept wearily down the ladder, and disappeared into the sea. A few bubbles rose where he sank. Some of the other slaves peered curiously over the side. At the prow of the galley sat a shark-charmer, beating monotonously upon a drum.

After some time the diver rose up out of the water, and clung panting to the ladder with a pearl in his right hand. The Negroes seized it from him, and thrust him back. The slaves fell asleep over their oars.

Again and again he came up, and each time that he did so he brought with him a beautiful pearl. The master of the galley weighed them, and put them into a little bag of green leather.

The young King tried to speak, hut his tongue seemed to cleave to the roof of his mouth, and his lips refused to move. The Negroes chattered to each other, and began to quarrel over a string of bright beads. Two cranes flew round and round the vessel.

Then the diver came up for the last time, and the pearl that he brought with him was fairer than all the pearls of Ormuz, for it was shaped like the full moon, and whiter than the morning star. But his face was strangely pale, and as he fell upon the deck the blood gushed from his ears and nostrils. He quivered for a little, and then he was still. The Negroes shrugged their shoulders, and threw the body overboard.

And the master of the galley laughed, and, reaching out, he took the pearl, and when he saw it he pressed it to his forehead and bowed. "It shall be," he said, "for the sceptre of the young King," and he made a sign to the Negroes to draw up the anchor.

And when the young King heard this he gave a great cry, and woke, and through the window he saw the long grey fingers of the dawn clutching at the fading stars.

And he fell asleep again, and dreamed, and this was his dream.

He thought that he was wandering through a dim wood, hung with strange fruits and with beautiful poisonous flowers. The adders hissed at him as he went by, and the bright parrots flew screaming from branch to branch. Huge tortoises lay asleep upon the hot mud. The trees were full of apes and peacocks.

On and on he went, till he reached the outskirts of the wood, and there he saw an immense multitude of men

toiling in the bed of a dried-up river. They swarmed up the crag like ants. They dug deep pits in the ground and went down into them. Some of them cleft the rocks with great axes; others grabbled in the sand. They tore up the cactus by its roots, and trampled on the scarlet blossoms. They hurried about, calling to each other, and no man was idle.

From the darkness of a cavern Death and Avarice watched them, and Death said, "I am weary; give me a third of them and let me go."

But Avarice shook her head. "They are my servants," she answered.

And Death said to her, "What hast thou in thy hand?

"I have three grains of corn," she answered; what is that to thee?"

"Give me one of them," cried Death, "to plant in my garden; only one of them, and I will go away."

"I will not give thee anything," said Avarice, and she hid her hand in the fold of her raiment.

And Death laughed, and took a cup, and dipped it into a pool of water, and out of the cup rose Ague. She passed through the great multitude, and a third of them lay dead. A cold mist followed her, and the watersnakes ran by her side.

And when Avarice saw that a third of the multitude was dead she beat her breast and wept. She beat her barren bosom, and cried aloud. "Thou hast slain a third of my servants," she cried, "get thee gone. There is war in the mountains of Tartary, and the kings of each side are calling to thee. The Afghans have slain the black ox, and are to battle. They have beaten upon their shields with their spears, and have put on their helmets of iron. What is my valley to thee, that thou should'st tarry in it? Get thee gone, and come here no more."

"Nay," answered Death, "but till thou hast given me a grain of corn I will not go."

But Avarice shut her hand, and clenched her teeth. "I will not give thee anything," she muttered.

And Death laughed, and took up a black stone, and threw it into the forest, and out of a thicket of wild hemlock came Fever in a robe of flame. She passed through the multitude, and touched them, and each man that she touched died. The grass withered beneath her feet as she walked.

And Avarice shuddered, and put ashes on her head. "Thou art cruel," she cried; "thou art cruel. There is famine in the walled cities of India, and the cisterns of Samarkand have run dry. There is famine in the walled cities of Egypt, and the locusts have come up from the desert. The Nile has not overflowed its banks, and the priests have cursed Isis and Osiris. Get thee gone to those who need thee, and leave me my servants."

"Nay," answered Death, "but till thou hast given me a grain of corn I will not go."

"I will not give thee anything," said Avarice.

And Death laughed again, and he whistled through his fingers, and a woman came flying through the air. Plague was written upon her forehead, and a crowd of lean vultures wheeled round her. She covered the valley with her wings, and no man was left alive.

And Avarice fled shrieking through the forest, and Death leaped upon his red horse and galloped away, and his galloping was faster than the wind.

And out of the slime at the bottom of the valley crept dragons and horrible things with scales, and the jackals came trotting along the sand, sniffing up the air with their nostrils.

And the young King wept, and said: "Who were these men and for what were they seeking?"

"For rubies for a king's crown," answered one who stood behind him.

And the young King started, and, turning round, he saw a man habited as a pilgrim and holding in his hand a mirror of silver.

And he grew pale, and said: "For what king?"

And the pilgrim answered: "Look in this mirror, and thou shalt see him."

And he looked in the mirror, and, seeing his own face, he gave a great cry and woke, and the bright sunlight was streaming into the room, and from the trees of the garden and pleasaunce the birds were singing.

And the Chamberlain and the high officers of State came in and made obeisance to him, and the pages brought him the robe of tissued gold, and set the crown and the sceptre before him.

And the young King looked at them, and they were beautiful. More beautiful were they than aught that he had ever seen. But he remembered his dreams, and he said to his lords: "Take these things away, for I will not wear them."

And the courtiers were amazed, and some of them laughed, for they thought that he was jesting.

But he spake sternly to them again, and said: "Take these things away, and hide them from me. Though it be the day of my coronation, I will not wear them. For on the loom of Sorrow, and by the white hands of Pain, has this my robe been woven. There is Blood in the heart of the ruby, and Death in the heart of the pearl." And he told them his three dreams.

And when the courtiers heard them they looked at each other and whispered, saying: "Surely he is mad; for what is a dream but a dream, and a vision but a vision? They are not real things that one should heed them. And what have we to do with the lives of those who toil for us? Shall a man not eat bread till he has seen the sower, nor drink wine till he has talked with the vinedresser?"

And the Chamberlain spake to the young King, and said, "My lord, I pray thee set aside these black thoughts of thine, and put on this fair robe, and set this crown upon thy head. For how shall the people know that thou art a king, if thou hast not a king's raiment?"

And the young King looked at him. "Is it so, indeed?" he questioned. "Will they not know me for a king if I have not a king's raiment?"

"They will not know thee, my lord," cried the Chamberlain.

"I had thought that there had been men who were kinglike," he answered, "but it may be as thou sayest. And yet I will not wear this robe, nor will I be crowned with this crown, but even as I came to the palace so will I go forth from it."

And he bade them all leave him, save one page whom he kept as his companion, a lad a year younger than himself. Him he kept for his service, and when he had bathed himself in clear water, he opened a great painted chest, and from it he took the leathern tunic and rough sheepskin cloak that he had worn when he had watched on the hillside the shaggy goats of the goatherd. These he put on, and in his hand he took his rude shepherd's staff.

And the little page opened his big blue eyes in wonder, and said smiling to him, "My lord, I see thy robe and thy sceptre, but where is thy crown?"

And the young King plucked a spray of wild briar that was climbing over the balcony, and bent it, and made a circlet of it, and set it on his own head.

"This shall be my crown," he answered.

And thus attired he passed out of his chamber into the Great Hall, where the nobles were waiting for him.

And the nobles made merry, and some of them cried out to him, "My lord, the people wait for their king, and thou showest them a beggar," and others were wroth and said, "He brings shame upon our state, and is unworthy to be our master." But he answered them not a word, but passed on, and went down the bright porphyry staircase, and out through the gates of bronze, and mounted upon his horse, and rode towards the cathedral, the little page running beside him.

And the people laughed and said, "It is the King's fool who is riding by," and they mocked him.

And he drew rein and said, "Nay, but I am the King." And he told them his three dreams.

And a man came out of the crowd and spake bitterly to him, and said, "Sir, knowest thou not that out of the luxury of the rich cometh the life of the poor? By your pomp we are nurtured, and your vices give us bread. To toil for a hard master is bitter, but to have no master to toil for is more bitter still. Thinkest thou that the ravens will feed us? And what cure hast thou for these things? Wilt thou say to the buyer, 'Thou shalt buy for so much,' and to the seller, 'Thou shalt sell at this price'? I trow not. Therefore go back to thy Palace and put on thy purple and fine linen. What hast thou to do with us, and what we suffer?"

"Are not the rich and the poor brothers?" asked the young King.

"Aye," answered the man, "and the name of the rich brother is Cain."

And the young King's eyes filled with tears, and he rode on through the murmurs of the people, and the little page grew afraid and left him.

And when he reached the great portal of the cathedral, the soldiers thrust their halberts out and said, "What dost thou seek here? None enters by this door but the King."

And his face flushed with anger, and he said to them, "I am the King," and waved their halberts aside and passed in.

And when the old Bishop saw him coming in his goatherd's dress, he rose up in wonder from his throne, and went to meet him, and said to him, "My son, is this a king's apparel? And with what crown shall I crown thee, and what sceptre shall I place in thy hand? Surely this should be to thee a day of joy, and not a day of abasement."

"Shall Joy wear what Grief has fashioned?" said the young King. And he told him his three dreams.

And when the Bishop had heard them he knit his brows, and said, "My son, I am an old man, and in the winter of my days, and I know that many evil things are done in the wide world. The fierce robbers come

down from the mountains, and carry off the little children, and sell them to the Moors. The lions lie in wait for the caravans, and leap upon the camels. The wild boar roots up the corn in the valley, and the foxes gnaw the vines upon the hill. The pirates lay waste the sea-coast and burn the ships of the fishermen, and take their nets from them. In the salt-marshes live the lepers; they have houses of wattled reeds, and none may come nigh them. The beggars wander through the cities, and eat their food with the dogs. Canst thou make these things not to be? Wilt thou take the leper for thy bedfellow, and set the beggar at thy board? Shall the lion do thy bidding, and the wild boar obey thee? Is not He who made misery wiser than thou art? Wherefore I praise thee not for this that thou hast done, but I bid thee ride back to the Palace and make thy face glad, and put on the raiment that beseemeth a king, and with the crown of gold I will crown thee, and the sceptre of pearl will I place in thy hand. And as for thy dreams, think no more of them. The burden of this world is too great for one man to bear, and the world's sorrow too heavy for one heart to suffer."

"Sayest thou that in this house?" said the young King, and he strode past the Bishop, and climbed up the steps of the altar, and stood before the image of Christ.

He stood before the image of Christ, and on his right hand and on his left were the marvellous vessels of gold, the chalice with the yellow wine, and the vial with the holy oil. He knelt before the image of Christ, and the great candles burned brightly by the jewelled shrine, and the smoke of the incense curled in thin blue wreaths through the dome. He bowed his head in prayer, and the priests in their stiff copes crept away from the altar.

And suddenly a wild tumult came from the street outside, and in entered the nobles with drawn swords and nodding plumes, and shields of polished steel.

"Where is this dreamer of dreams?" they cried. "Where is this King, who is apparelled like a beggar – this boy who brings shame upon our state? Surely we will slay him, for he is unworthy to rule over us."

And the young King bowed his head again, and prayed, and when he had finished his prayer he rose up, and turning round he looked at them sadly.

And lo! through the painted windows came the sunlight streaming upon him, and the sunbeams wove round him a tissued robe that was fairer than the robe that had been fashioned for his pleasure. The dead staff blossomed, and bore lilies that were whiter than pearls. The dry thorn blossomed, and bore roses that were redder than rubies. Whiter than fine pearls were the lilies, and their stems were of bright silver. Redder than male rubies were the roses, and their leaves were of beaten gold.

He stood there in the raiment of a king, and the gates of the jewelled shrine flew open, and from the crystal of the many-rayed monstrance shone a marvellous and mystical light. He stood there in a king's raiment, and the Glory of God filled the place, and the saints in their carven niches seemed to move. In the fair raiment of a king he stood before them, and the organ pealed out its music, and the trumpeters blew upon their trumpets, and the singing boys sang.

And the people fell upon their knees in awe, and the nobles sheathed their swords and did homage, and the Bishop's face grew pale, and his hands trembled. "A greater than I hath crowned thee," he cried, and he knelt before him.

And the young King came down from the high altar, and passed home through the midst of the people. But no man dared look upon his face, for it was like the face of an angel.

THE HAPPY PRINCE

HIGH ABOVE the city, on a tall column, stood the statue of the Happy Prince. He was gilded all over with thin leaves of fine gold, for eyes he had two bright sapphires, and a large red ruby glowed on his sword-hilt.

He was very much admired indeed. "He is as beautiful as a weathercock," remarked one of the Town Councillors who wished to gain a reputation for having artistic tastes; "only not quite so useful," he added, fearing lest people should think him unpractical, which he really was not.

"Why can't you be like the Happy Prince?" asked a sensible mother of her little boy who was crying for the moon. "The Happy Prince never dreams of crying for anything."

"I am glad there is some one in the world who is quite happy," muttered a disappointed man as he gazed at the wonderful statue.

"He looks just like an angel," said the Charity Children as they came out of the cathedral in their bright scarlet cloaks, and their clean white pinafores.

"How do you know?" said the Mathematical Master, "you have never seen one."

"Ah! but we have, in our dreams," answered the children; and the Mathematical Master frowned and looked very severe, for he did not approve of children dreaming.

One night there flew over the city a little Swallow. His friends had gone away to Egypt six weeks before, but he had stayed behind, for he was in love with the most beautiful Reed. He had met her early in the spring as he was flying down the river after a big yellow moth, and had been so attracted by her slender waist that he had stopped to talk to her.

"Shall I love you?" said the Swallow, who liked to come to the point at once, and the Reed made him a low bow. So he flew round and round her, touching the water with his wings, and making silver ripples. This was his courtship, and it lasted all through the summer.

"It is a ridiculous attachment," twittered the other

Swallows, "she has no money, and far too many relations;" and indeed the river was quite full of Reeds. Then, when the autumn came, they all flew away.

After they had gone he felt lonely, and began to tire of his lady-love. "She has no conversation," he said, "and I am afraid that she is a coquette, for she is always flirting with the wind." And certainly, whenever the wind blew, the Reed made the most graceful curtsies. "I admit that she is domestic," he continued, "but I love travelling, and my wife, consequently, should love travelling also."

"Will you come away with me?" he said finally to her; but the Reed shook her head, she was so attached to her home.

"You have been trifling with me," he cried, "I am off to the Pyramids. Good-bye!" and he flew away.

All day long he flew, and at night-time he arrived at the city. "Where shall I put up?" he said; "I hope the town has made preparations."

Then he saw the statue on the tall column. "I will put up there," he cried; "it is a fine position with plenty of fresh air." So he alighted just between the feet of the Happy Prince.

"I have a golden bedroom," he said softly to himself as he looked round, and he prepared to go to sleep; but just as he was putting his head under his wing a large drop of water fell on him. "What a curious thing!" he cried, "there is not a single cloud in the sky, the stars are quite clear and bright, and yet it is raining. The climate in the north of Europe is really dreadful. The Reed used to like the rain, but that was merely her selfishness."

Then another drop fell.

"What is the use of a statue if it cannot keep the rain off?" he said; "I must look for a good chimney-pot," and he determined to fly away.

But before he had opened his wings, a third drop fell, and he looked up, and saw – Ah! what did he see?

The eyes of the Happy Prince were filled with tears, and tears were running down his golden cheeks. His face was so beautiful in the moonlight that the little Swallow was filled with pity.

"Who are you?" he said.

"I am the Happy Prince."

"Why are you weeping then?" asked the Swallow; "you have quite drenched me."

"When I was alive and had a human heart," answered the statue, "I did not know what tears were, for I lived in the Palace of Sans-Souci, where sorrow is not allowed to enter. In the daytime I played with my companions in the garden, and in the

evening I led the dance in the Great Hall. Round the garden ran a very lofty wall, but I never cared to ask what lay beyond it, everything about me was so beautiful. My courtiers called me the Happy Prince, and happy indeed I was, if pleasure be happiness. So I lived, and so I died. And now that I am dead they have set me up here so high that I can see all the ugliness and all the misery of my city, and though my heart is made of lead yet I cannot choose but weep."

"What, is he not solid gold?" said the Swallow to himself. He was too polite to make any personal remarks out loud.

"Far away," continued the statue in a low musical voice, "far away in a little street there is a poor house. One of the windows is open, and through it I can see a woman seated at a table. Her face is thin and worn, and she has coarse, red hands, all pricked by the needle, for she is a seamstress. She is embroidering passion-flowers on a satin gown for the loveliest of the Queen's maids-of-honour to wear at the next Court-ball. In a bed in the corner of the room her little boy is lying ill. He has a fever, and is asking for oranges. His mother has nothing to give him but river water, so he is crying. Swallow, Swallow, little Swallow, will you not bring her the ruby out of my sword-hilt? My feet are fastened to this pedestal and I cannot move."

"I am waited for in Egypt," said the Swallow. "My friends are flying up and down the Nile, and talking to the large lotus-flowers. Soon they will go to sleep in the tomb of the great King. The King is there himself in his painted coffin. He is wrapped in yellow linen, and embalmed with spices. Round his neck is a chain of pale green jade, and his hands are like withered leaves."

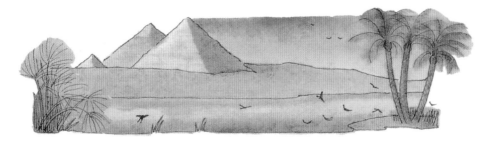

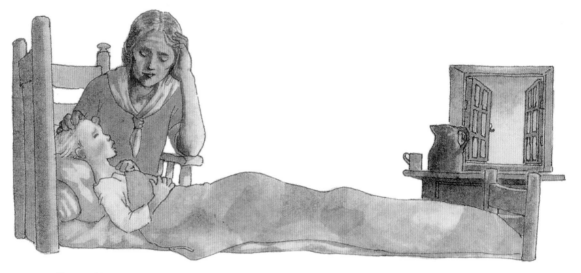

"Swallow, Swallow, little Swallow," said the Prince, "will you not stay with me for one night, and be my messenger? The boy is so thirsty, and the mother so sad."

"I don't think I like boys," answered the Swallow. "Last summer, when I was staying on the river, there were two rude boys, the miller's sons, who were always throwing stones at me. They never hit me, of course; we swallows fly far too well for that, and besides, I come of a family famous for its agility; but still, it was a mark of disrespect."

But the Happy Prince looked so sad that the little Swallow was sorry. "It is very cold here," he said; "but I will stay with you for one night, and be your messenger."

"Thank you, little Swallow," said the Prince.

So the Swallow picked out the great ruby from the Prince's sword, and flew away with it in his beak over the roofs of the town.

He passed by the cathedral tower, where the white marble angels were sculptured. He passed by the palace and heard the sound of dancing. A beautiful girl came out on the balcony with her lover. "How wonderful the stars are," he said to her, "and how wonderful is the power of love!"

"I hope my dress will be ready in time for the State-ball," she answered; "I have ordered passion-flowers to be embroidered on it; but the seamstresses are so lazy."

He passed over the river, and saw the lanterns hanging to the masts of the ships. He passed over the Ghetto, and saw the old Jews bargaining with each other, and weighing out money in copper scales. At last he came to the poor house and looked in. The boy was tossing feverishly on his bed, and the mother had fallen asleep, she was so tired. In he hopped, and laid the great ruby on the table beside the woman's thimble. Then he flew gently round the bed, fanning the boy's forehead with his wings. "How cool I feel," said the boy, "I must be getting better;" and he sank into a delicious slumber.

Then the Swallow flew back to the Happy Prince, and told him what he had done. "It is curious," he remarked, "but I feel quite warm now, although it is so cold."

"That is because you have done a good action," said the Prince. And the little Swallow began to think, and then he fell asleep. Thinking always made him sleepy.

When day broke he flew down to the river and had a bath. "What a remarkable phenomenon," said the Professor of Ornithology as he was passing over the bridge. "A swallow in winter!" And he wrote a long letter about it to the local newspaper. Every one quoted it, it was full of so many words that they could not understand.

"To-night I go to Egypt," said the Swallow, and he was in high spirits at the prospect. He visited all the public monuments, and sat a long time on top of the church steeple. Wherever he went the Sparrows chirruped, and said to each other, "What a distinguished stranger!" so he enjoyed himself very much.

When the moon rose he flew back to the Happy Prince. "Have you any commissions for Egypt?" he cried; "I am just starting."

"Swallow, Swallow, little Swallow," said the Prince, "will you not stay with me one night longer?"

"I am waited for in Egypt," answered the Swallow. "Tomorrow my friends will fly up to the Second Cataract. The river-horse couches there among the bulrushes, and on a great granite throne sits the God Memnon. All night long he watches the stars, and when the morning star shines he utters one cry of joy, and then he is silent. At noon the yellow lions come down to the water's edge to drink. They have eyes like green beryls, and their roar is louder than the roar of the cataract."

"Swallow, Swallow, little Swallow," said the Prince, "far away across the city I see a young man in a garret. He is leaning over a desk covered with papers, and in a tumbler by his side there is a bunch of withered violets. His hair is brown and crisp, and his lips are red as a pomegranate, and he has large and dreamy eyes. He is trying to finish a play for the Director of the Theatre, but he is too cold to write any more. There is no fire in the grate, and hunger has made him faint."

"I will wait with you one night longer," said the Swallow, who really had a good heart. "Shall I take him another ruby?"

"Alas! I have no ruby now," said the Prince; "my eyes are all that I have left. They are made of rare sapphires, which were brought out of India a thousand years ago. Pluck out one of them and take it to him. He will sell it to the jeweller, and buy food and firewood, and finish his play."

"Dear Prince," said the Swallow, "I cannot do that;" and he began to weep.

"Swallow, Swallow, little Swallow," said the Prince, "do as I command you."

So the Swallow plucked out the Prince's eye, and flew away to the student's garret. It was easy enough to get in, as there was a hole in the roof. Through this he darted, and came into the room. The young man had his head buried in his hands, so he did not

hear the flutter of the bird's wings, and when he looked up he found the beautiful sapphire lying on the withered violets.

"I am beginning to be appreciated," he cried; "this is from some great admirer. Now I can finish my play," and he looked quite happy.

The next day the Swallow flew down to the harbour. He sat on the mast of a large vessel and watched the sailors hauling big chests out of the hold with ropes. "Heave a-hoy!" they shouted as each chest came up. "I am going to Egypt!" cried the Swallow, but nobody minded, and when the moon rose he flew back to the Happy Prince.

"I am come to bid you good-bye," he cried.

"Swallow, Swallow, little Swallow," said the Prince, "will you not stay with me one night longer?"

"It is winter," answered the Swallow, "and the chill snow will soon be here. In Egypt the sun is warm on the green palm trees, and the crocodiles lie in the mud and look lazily about them. My companions are building a nest in the Temple of Baalbec, and the pink and white doves are watching them, and cooing to each other. Dear Prince, I must leave you, but I will never forget you, and next spring I will bring you back two beautiful jewels in place of those you have given away. The ruby shall be redder than a red rose, and the sapphire shall be as blue as the great sea."

"In the square below," said the Happy Prince, "there stands a little match-girl. She has let her matches fall in the gutter, and they are all spoiled. Her father will beat her if she does not bring home some money, and she is crying. She has no shoes or stockings, and her little head is bare. Pluck out my other eye, and give it to her, and her father will not beat her."

"I will stay with you one night longer," said the Swallow, "but I cannot pluck out your eye. You would be quite blind then."

"Swallow, Swallow, little Swallow," said the Prince, "do as I command you."

So he plucked out the Prince's other eye, and darted down with it. He swooped past the match-girl, and slipped the jewel into the palm of her hand. "What a lovely bit of glass," cried the little girl; and she ran home, laughing.

Then the Swallow came back to the Prince. "You are blind now," he said, "so I will stay with you always."

"No, little Swallow," said the poor Prince, "you must go away to Egypt."

"I will stay with you always," said the Swallow, and he slept at the Prince's feet.

All the next day he sat on the Prince's shoulder, and told him stories of what he had seen in strange lands. He told him of the red ibises, who stand in long rows on the banks of the Nile, and catch gold fish in their beaks; of the Sphinx, who is as old as the world itself, and lives in the desert, and knows everything; of the merchants, who walk slowly by the side of their camels, and carry amber beads in their hands; of the King of the Mountains of the Moon, who is as black as ebony, and worships a large crystal; of the great green snake that sleeps in a palm-tree, and has twenty priests to feed it with honey-cakes; and of the pygmies who sail over a big lake on large flat leaves, and are always at war with the butterflies.

"Dear little Swallow," said the Prince, "you tell me of marvellous things, but more marvellous than anything is the suffering of men and of women. There is no Mystery so great as Misery. Fly over my city, little Swallow, and tell me what you see there."

So the Swallow flew over the great city, and saw the rich making merry in their beautiful houses, while the beggars were sitting at the gates. He flew into dark lanes, and saw the white faces of starving children looking out listlessly at the black streets. Under the archway of a bridge two little boys were lying in one another's arms to try and keep themselves warm. "How hungry we are!" they said. "You must not lie here," shouted the Watchman, and they wandered out into the rain.

Then he flew back and told the Prince what he had seen.

"I am covered with fine gold," said the Prince, "you must take it off, leaf by leaf, and give it to my poor; the living always think that gold can make them happy."

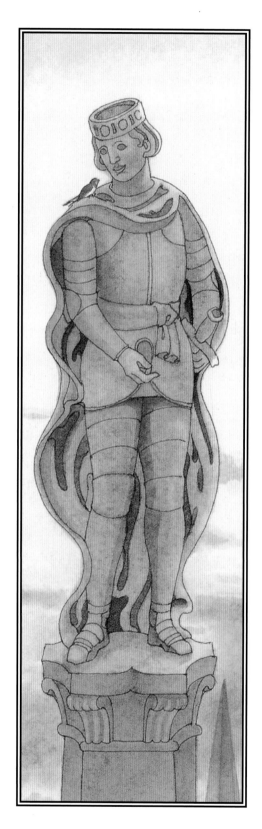

Leaf after leaf of the fine gold the Swallow picked off, till the Happy Prince looked quite dull and grey. Leaf after leaf of the fine gold he brought to the poor, and the children's faces grew rosier, and they laughed and played games in the street. "We have bread now!" they cried.

Then the snow came, and after the snow came the frost. The streets looked as if they were made of silver, they were so bright and glistening; long icicles like crystal daggers hung down from the eaves of the houses, everybody went about in furs, and the little boys wore scarlet caps and skated on the ice.

The poor little Swallow grew colder and colder, but he would not leave the Prince, he loved him too well. He picked up crumbs outside the baker's door when the baker was not looking, and tried to keep himself warm by flapping his wings.

But at last he knew that he was going to die. He had just strength to fly up to the Prince's shoulder once more. "Good-bye, dear Prince!" he murmured, "will you let me kiss your hand?"

"I am glad that you are going to Egypt at last, little Swallow," said the Prince, "you have stayed too long here; but you must kiss me on the lips, for I love you."

"It is not to Egypt that I am going," said the Swallow. "I am going to the House of Death. Death is the brother of Sleep, is he not?"

And he kissed the Happy Prince on the lips, and fell down dead at his feet.

At that moment a curious crack sounded inside the statue, as if something had broken. The fact is that the leaden heart had snapped right in two. It certainly was a dreadfully hard frost.

Early the next morning the Mayor was walking in the square below in company with the Town Councillors. As they passed the column he looked up at the statue: "Dear me! how shabby the Happy Prince looks!" he said.

"How shabby indeed!" cried the Town Councillors, who always agreed with the Mayor, and they went up to look at it.

"The ruby has fallen out of his sword, his eyes are gone, and he is golden no longer," said the Mayor; "in fact, he is little better than a beggar!"

"Little better than a beggar," said the Town Councillors.

"And here is actually a dead bird at his feet!" continued the Mayor. "We must really issue a proclamation that birds are not to be allowed to die here." And the Town Clerk made a note of the suggestion.

So they pulled down the statue of the Happy Prince. "As he is no longer beautiful he is no longer useful," said the Art Professor at the University.

Then they melted the statue in a furnace, and the Mayor held a meeting of the Corporation to decide what was to be done with the metal. "We must have another statue, of course," he said, "and it shall be a statue of myself."

"Of myself," said each of the Town Councillors, and they quarrelled. When I last heard of them they were quarrelling still.

"What a strange thing!" said the overseer of the workmen at the foundry. "This broken lead heart will not melt in the furnace. We must throw it away." So they threw it on a dust-heap where the dead Swallow was also lying.

"Bring me the two most precious things in the city," said God to one of His Angels; and the Angel brought Him the leaden heart and the dead bird.

"You have rightly chosen," said God, "for in my garden of Paradise this little bird shall sing for evermore, and in my city of gold the Happy Prince shall praise me."